PRAISE FOR EILEEN MYLES AND *I MUST BE LIVING TWICE*

"The voice of Eileen Myles is a phenomenon of unforced and world-altering vigor—like Rimbaud's, maybe, but with more swerve, more grit, more minerality. Be grateful that you've coincided with her on earth and can receive firsthand these brilliant, funny, tuneful poems—a reckless new kind of melody, with leaps and tempo changes and atonalities of urgent truthfulness. Her urban pastorals pay strict attention to weather, heartbreak, animals, shock, moodswing, interruption, coincidence, noise, and the clarity of the ordinary, sped up to resemble dialectical dynamite. Myles's poems come disguised as photographs but are actually transfigurations, reality's usual arrangements turned inside out. The sharpness of her intellect is matched by the quick, terse, idiomatic way she exercises her lyrical powers. *I Must Be Living Twice* is a landmark to revere and love." —Wayne Koestenbaum

"If trees could walk, if dogs could talk, if bees could explain and pigeons spin over the Endless Cities of Eileen, they would be her best friends in the end. The lady is a tramp with a lonely quill in her hand and a tree's bark to write on. More spirit than flesh, more beast than man, you'll see this in the poems, the beautiful poems." —Fanny Howe

"Eileen Myles's *I Must Be Living Twice* is as heartbreaking as it is generous and uplifting. These poems are written with a certain tender affection for the human experience that could only be conveyed through Myles's careful, yet effortlessly flowing prose." —Mira Gonzalez

"Five thousand years from now people will still be reading Eileen Myles. To assume what she assumes is the real substance of divine inspiration: how to be in your body and sing to your soul, how to fall in and out of love, to find out that hell is real and to go there, to learn the true meaning of heaven, romance, intoxication and sacred daring—in short, as it turns out, what it feels like to be a fucking god. Everything Orpheus, Sappho, and Dante knew, she knows, and more." —Ariana Reines

"For a taste, lick, touch, smell, jam on living in New York 1975 and onwards, getting right to it from her gut, vagina, brain. . . . Freed in poetry. . . . Read this, Eileen is epic!" —Kim Gordon

ALSO BY EILEEN MYLES

Snowflake / different streets

Inferno (a poet's novel)

The Importance of Being Iceland / travel essays in art

Sorry, Tree

Tow (with drawings by artist Larry C. Collins)

Skies

on my way

Cool for You

School of Fish

Maxfield Parrish / early & new poems

The New Fuck You / adventures in lesbian reading
  (with Liz Kotz)

Not Me

1969

Bread and Water

Sappho's Boat

A Fresh Young Voice from the Plains

Polar Ode (with Anne Waldman)

The Irony of the Leash

I MUST BE LIVING TWICE

NEW & SELECTED POEMS

1975–2014

EILEEN MYLES

ecco

An Imprint of HarperCollinsPublishers

HarperCollins books may be purchased for educational, business, or sales promotional use. For information please e-mail the Special Markets Department at SPsales@harpercollins.com.

FIRST EDITION

Designed by Suet Yee Chong

Library of Congress Cataloging-in-Publication Data has been applied for.

ISBN 978-0-06-238908-4

15 16 17 18 19   OV/RRD   10 9 8 7 6 5 4 3

FOR MAGGIE

CONTENTS

NEW POEMS

What Tree Am I Waiting   3
Summer   5
Prophesy   6
LONDON
EXCHANGE   7
My Devil   10
memory   13
That Rat's Death   14

THE IRONY OF THE LEASH (1978)

Homebody   23
An Attitude About Poetry   24
Evening   25
Subscription   26
The Irony of the Leash   27

A FRESH YOUNG VOICE FROM THE PLAINS (1981)

The Honey Bear   35
Along the Strand   36
Greece   40
Skuppy the Sailor Dog   41
medium poem   42
Welsh Poetry   43
My Cheap Lifestyle   44
On the Death of Robert Lowell   45
Texas   46

SAPPHO'S BOAT (1982)

Joan   49
"Romantic Pain"   51
La Vita Nuova   56
Exploding the Spring Mystique   58

My Rampant Muse, for Her   61

Whax 'n Wayne   62

Yellow Tulips   67

New York Tulips   68

Lorna & Vicki   69

NOT ME (1991)

A Poem   75

Edward the Confessor   78

Holes   82

April Noon   85

The Sadness of Leaving   86

Hot Night   89

And Then The Weather Arrives   97

November   99

New England Wind   101

Mad Pepper   102

The Sad Part Is   106

Triangles of Power   107

Peanut Butter   109

The Real Drive   113

Autumn in New York   117

Mal Maison   118

An American Poem   134

MAXFIELD PARRISH (1995)

Maxfield Parrish   141

Bleeding Hearts   145

Sleepless   147

"I always put my pussy . . ."   150

SHHH   152

The Mirror Is My Mother   153

En Garde   155

PV   159

Looking Out, a Sailor   162

A Debate With A Glove   169

Late March   172

You   174

"No Poems"   176

Life   180

The Poet   183

SCHOOL OF FISH (1997)

School of Fish   187

Road Warrior   189

Last Supper   190

Merk   193

Porn Poems   198

Just God   199

Mr. Twenty   201

Aurora   205

Woo   207

Rotting Symbols   208

Sullivan's Brain   211

My War Is Love   215

Waterfall   218

Tonight   219

Story   221

No No   222

SKIES (2001)

"Jonathan's . . ."   225

"The whole mess . . ."   227

My Wife Is Shopping   230

"Twenty years ago . . ."   232

Writing   234

"My mind's . . ."   236

The Center   237

Milk   240

And   242

Snakes   243
Infinity Mini   246
Mt. St. Helens   250
"I don't know . . ."   252
My Hat   253
Weather   255
Sympathy   256
Bone   258
The Guest   260

ON MY WAY (2001)

Harmonica   271
Scribner's   273

SORRY, TREE (2007)

No Rewriting   279
For Jordana   285
Each Defeat   287
unnamed New York   289
April 5   291
That Country   293
I'm moved   296
San Diego Poem   298
cigarette girl   299
To Hell   301

SNOWFLAKE / DIFFERENT STREETS (2012)

Transitions   307
Snowflake   311
D.H.   314
Choke   315
Caesarean Toothbrush   317
"The cat is in . . ."   319
Your Name   320

Mitten   322

Hi   324

The Weather   326

Smile   329

The Perfect Faceless Fish   330

My Box   336

EPILOGUE

Anonymous   341

Twice (essay)   343

Acknowledgments   355

New Poems

WHAT TREE AM I WAITING

That whole part of the world
where I won't go any-
more
that whole separation
that I won't feel
high in this house
in this hemisphere
in this artificial light
that is artificial
in the earliest morning; dark
in pages and pens
in an unfamiliar bed
in the foot curl
furniture
each rumble
when morning comes
and it's still morning
and it's still night
I married a dead girl
we were born in her
bloom
remember that fat bumblebee
landed on a lamp
I opened the doors
and I forgot and the house
got colder and colder
where is this house
the seam between boards
merely gains my attention
it's dark and thin
I monitor each situation
my bladder growing full
climb down climb up
what tree am I waiting

my whole life in weather
waiting for my raft
I'll fly to another island
I'll take a train
already I know
it will hurt
this is the hurt country
I came here
to hold the hurt like a bird
like a tree
traffic has rings
we watch it whirl around
damaging our night
great continents hold
the feelings and the ages
what is mine
going blind
great masses of them
not going home
the country drew a line
because of memory
one said
I feel my heart race ahead
in eternity there is this ache
there is this wakefulness

SUMMER

That morning in the light
that television show got born
I remember it in California
every morning a show
and her wife in bed
do I like her being there
but I have this now
my pride and my telephone
and all my information

PROPHESY

I'm playing with the devil's cock
it's like a crayon
it's like a fat burnt crayon
I'm writing a poem with it
I'm writing that down
all that rattling heat in this room
I'm using that
I'm using that tingling rattle
that light in the middle of the room
it's my host
I've always been afraid of you
scared you're god and something else
I'm afraid when you're yellow
tawny
white it's okay. Transparent cool
you don't look like home
my belly is homeless
flopping over the waist of my jeans like an omelette
there better be something about feeling fat
what there really is is a lack of emptiness
I'm aiming for that empty feeling
going to get some of that
and then I'll be back

LONDON
EXCHANGE

I have utmost
respect for you
but in that
moment if I
were to
get out of
your way
instead of
walking up the stairs
to my home
I would have
no respect
for myself.
I didn't know
why you couldn't
understand this
when I told
you. Instead
you screamed
at me and
told me I
was rude. And
then you
said someone
of my
age should
know meaning
that you
were adding
to my crime
the fact
that I am

older than you.
What am I
to do. How
many days
have passed
and I
have no
reason to think
that
your ancestors
were stolen
from their
home in A-
frica
and because
of my not
knowing that this
is true
but thinking
that it
is possible
it makes
me certain
that respect
next time
would be
for me
to step around.
Maybe
I could say
quietly joining you
for a moment
in your

vast and
ancient
sorrow
that was
my home

MY DEVIL

before the sky
opens &
I drop my
tiny ladder
I will inhabit
the minds
of dogs
& try me on
for size
I will lean
against the side
of the bldg.
& smoke my
blonde smoke
I will be
Inside my
big car
something happens
that's what
I say
there's always
a recipe
I will recite
My blonde
list
I am
the negation
of you
spell's on
they're reeling us
in
I want her
thoughts
These cattle

are mine
the salad's
not bad
The devil is
Turning into ev-
eryone
I'm you for
a while. Genitals
itchy. That's
me. I'm going
to ruin
your corn
it's not such
a bad idea.
Give me that
poem. Give
me that menu
give me
key
I don't
need to
come or go
I'm there
In your prayer.
Mr. President
consider the
wish of the
tiny child.
he is me.
does it taste good
or does it look
like it tastes good
you don't know.
See.

MEMORY

I lost it
that soft
ball I threw
in my room
across
many walls
because
I love toys.

It warmed
to my grip
became dirty
went splat
and I threw
it against
the writing
on the wall
not hitting
it exactly
but with
a smile
went
out the door
to rise over
golden hills
and descend
with a family
on a tram
ride through
graves
you irreplace-
able
the best
thing I had

my passion
for you
I hope
will continue,
summer

THAT RAT'S DEATH

I'm proud
that I fed my avocado
to the mice this
week

To see that scattered dust
around the hole

I felt dis-
appointed the apple had
been spared
the throbbing
soup, home

he said it's a storm
it's a storm I thought
am I allowed
to ask entire questions
to take this
space alone

you bobbing
you painted in my dog's
face so care-
fully

some kind of violence
stretches the thought so
long and allows the horns
of words to touch each
other. I think of him

taking
this much space.

you don't know about this
dish towel
for that matter

who was I in another time
giving the tails so much

puzzled that these spices
went someplace else
they did today in a sandwich

the empty hall into which I am
reading
the empty country
an entire country
I wanted all of them

how I would like
just one to pick
things up in
its cities and its rain
its coast
the outer coat

78 rpm
silly
news-
papers
turning
cat on a porch
and other countries
nearby
& home ready for me
when I have

something to say or
show

if ever
my empty mistakes
my empty vase
my empty powers of horror
my empty sex

o bring the snow

that rat's death
killed me because i
would see it for days
over and over and
it hardly could be the same
rat whose insides
whisked the street

we don't think that war
is such an incredible
mess but it was
just yesterday
and in ancient poems
years ago in the past

dying the balloon just
bursts it cannot

bring u back again

the huge cool breath
the lake doesn't want
you anymore or her

arms her sweet
muff or breast the storm
the past.

but no I won't leave
my cheese out for them
anymore and I must be
the last person in the world
in new york to read him
who told us about mice

that sing & fill empty auditoriums
like us and our singing hearts
our formula for bringing
it out. Pulling the receptacle
apart watch the tiny ship
floating on it
smithereens

I ducked the tail edging over

taking a little bit more. The price
of wider concepts is not
choosing your drops oh
flicking me off reminding
me of you everyone yell at once

Two Rabbit legs jutting out

I keep my childhood
around almost more than every-
one and a mouse can share
my house wet toot tootsie

it's kind of great the whole
thing is relative. Since I ad-
mired his mountains I imagin-
ed I was in his landscapes

but opening packages is occurring
all over the place. That's a
strong image and I feel like
the smallness is directly rooted

forgetting to use the new cal-
endar I planned. These
marks (I imagined) are the sources

all the milk flooding wildly
over the rolling hills and out of
the sun's comical eyes. Not tears
but creamy drops
of mammalian weather.

I'm given real information
and the most difficult part
is blindly creating the space
where the parts I can't
see or even hear spread out
(like the night in Paris when
I walked to the movies
) onto my desk and the surrounding
hills into the bleachers where everyone
is pounding themselves bloody
in salute of the hunt

all I ever wanted was dinner
or at least his
love the delight I see

in him is equally empty for anyone
& probably that's his
stealth. Inner lake. There's a car a maroon
a colourless oval I can imagine the
seats and the feeling of hearing
a song as we're weaving
over hills. There's no break. Ev-
erybody I ever saw in my
seacoast community is already
facing the problems huge and
gloomy I grant you and the
night spills on my keys which
are splayed over the counter and
outside it's light. & they are flip-
ping their cards every one of
them.

The Irony of the Leash

1978

HOMEBODY

Oh, Hello. C'mon in.
You know I was just thinking about how you've
Always thought I was <u>cool</u> . . .
And here I am, cooking fishcakes and broccoli.
I didn't know how I could re-present all this for you.
This is where I'm really at. Nothing's
As fetching as the raw.
I heard the dog barking on the third landing
& I was fairly sure it'd be you.
Kind of rainy out tonight. I was so exhausted
After work. Made some coffee
& sat here reading the Voice. Sort of
Thought I'd hear from you. I thought,
Well, he'll either be in the same mood
Or different. And look:
I've got a magenta sock and a rust
Sock on. Just like the, uh, Futurists.
And my old work shirt. Feels good
Since it's clean for a change.
Oh, do you want some? The broccoli's
Good with the grated cheese on it. Yeah,
The fishcakes suck,
But just douse them with lemon juice.

AN ATTITUDE ABOUT POETRY

My attitude about poetry is somewhat
this, I should be doing something
that pays more money,
I love comfort, bright things for myself
and the ability to splurge on people I
like, to be able to dislike
people who have bucks

That is the poetry of money.
Money is a friend,
a comfy chair when you need to sit,
free walking. Buying rides.
Zoom in on this one.
Avoid that one in a helicopter ride
around Australia. Bury
my sorrows in an incredible meal.
You like that star. I buy you that car.
Never drunk but gliding on the
      ethers of everyone's
        drunkenness.
        It trips me up,
my lightweight love of cash,
    it clicks on my teeth.
      My words jingle.

EVENING

Supposed to be there at 7 o'clock.
It's 8 o'clock now. Better buy some beer.
Go to the door, Sorry I'm late Frank
Here's six apologies . . .

Sit down at the table start drinking my words
Start playing Parcheesi with his kid.
Who keeps revising the rules, the little cheat.
Keeps using my lighter. It's cheap
But so what . . . he's irritating me.
We have some dinner, some steak, some rice,
(Call broccoli <u>trees</u>.)

Call the situation perfunctory and sweet.
We go look at poems, postcards, we
Drink coffee but the beer is still with us,

Wish I had some grass, wish I was someplace
                                        else

Boring to be me, glad I'm not married,
I'd be a child-beater, glad I can go home.
I feel woozy,

                    Walk down

Gorgeous soft tree-lined streets in the
Dark. Cushy. As the dark rows of trees
Are stroking the wind or
The wind's stroking them.

SUBSCRIPTION

Animals forever escaping
from zoos
& they will come to my door.
Too many masturbation manuals
are being written. Too much pie
passes over the counter. I bathe
in yellow light & dream of you.
I miss myself as the train
pulls out of a station in Jerez, España.

THE IRONY OF THE LEASH

Life is a plot to make me move.
I fill its forms, an unwitting
                    crayon

        I am prey to the materials
of me, combinations
        create me into something
        else, civilization's inventions

numb me, placate me
                carry me around. I
am no better than a dog.
        My terms are not bark
                and howl

but I often get drunk and rau-
cous, often I need to get
laid so bad I imagine my
howls lighting up the neighborhood
                pasting rings
                around the moon.

As a child I was very in love
with the stars. As a human
        a victim of my perceptions
it is natural that I should love
light and as a passive dreamer

it is natural that I should be attracted
to the most distant inaccessible
light. What do you make of
this. Friend? I need the reass-
                        urance

of human voices so I live with
a phone or I go out and seek
my friends. Now they are always
different, these people who
happen to be moved by the same
            music as me, whose
faces I like, good voices,

I can recognize the oncoming footsteps
of a person I like. In this
I am little better than a dog.

Sometimes I go to the movies and I
sit in the dark. Leaving the light
and relishing the movements
            of images occurring
         in another time, bright
and pretty, and though I know
very well,
    (as I paid my 1.50 and came
in here and chose a seat
a decision based on the condition
of my eyesight and my place
         in society
I may sit in the front or
the back, am I old,
      am I young . . .)

I know very well that this movie is not
   real, yet I am often
in the grips of fears more real
than those my own life throws up
for my unwilling complicity

and I am visibly shaken, often
        nearly screaming with fright
and revulsion . . .

                yet I know it is not real.

Movies have caused me to become
an artist. I guess I simply
        believe that life is not
        enough. I spin dreams
of the quotidian out of words I
could not help but choose.

They reflect my educational background,
    the economic situation of
            my parents and the countries
their parents came from. My words
        are also chemical reflections:

metabolically I am either fast or
        slow, like short words or
        long ones, sometimes I
like words which clack hard against
    each other like a line of
            wooden trains. Sometimes
I wish my words would meld
to a single glowing plastic tube slightly
        defying time.   I write
quite a bit,

        I no longer believe in religion
but find writing an admirable
            substitute,
I don't particularly believe in art

but I know that unless there is
     something I do which is
at least as artificial and snide
                    and self-perpetuating . . .

well then I would have to find
someone else who
     had that sort of handle
on things and hold onto him
     for dear life.

I would be less than a dog.
I think it's important to have
     your own grip on
things, however
that works and then you should
pursue that and spend the
     rest of the time
doing the ordinary.

Exactly like a dog. Dogs
are friendly creatures unless
   they've been mistreated.
They like to eat and run around.
They neither drink nor smoke
nor take drugs. They are perfect.
          They mate freely
whenever they have the urge.
They piss and shit according to
their needs, often they appear
to be smiling but of course
they are always happy.
Interestingly enough,
it is quite popular, particularly

in the city in which I live,
to own a dog, to walk him on a
                              leash
morning noon and night, people with
families have dogs and they add
        to the general abundant chaos
        of the household,

people who live alone own dogs. For
protection, regularity and
the general sense of owning a friend.
People love their dogs and undoubtedly
their dogs love them. Though
they are faithless and impersonal.
They love their owners because
they feed them, stroke them,
bring them outside to run around,

        if a dog gets injured
its owner will take it to a doctor or
a clinic, depending on the economic
        situation of the owner.

Dogs do not believe in God or Art.
Intrinsically they have a grip
        on things.

I unfortunately do not. I sit
here with a bottle of beer, a cigarette
        and my latest poem, The Irony of the Leash.

August 6

A Fresh Young Voice
from the Plains
1981

THE HONEY BEAR

Billie Holiday was on the radio
I was standing in the kitchen
smoking my cigarette of this
pack I plan to finish tonight
last night of smoking youth.
I made a cup of this funny
kind of tea I've had hanging
around. A little too sweet
an odd mix. My only impulse
was to make it sweeter.
Ivy Anderson was singing
pretty late tonight
in my very bright kitchen.
I'm standing by the tub
feeling a little older
nearly thirty in my very
bright kitchen tonight.
I'm not a bad looking woman
I suppose   O it's very quiet
in my kitchen tonight   I'm squeezing
this plastic honey bear   a noodle
of honey dripping into the odd sweet
tea. It's pretty late
Honey Bear's cover was loose
and somehow honey   dripping down
the bear's face catching
in the crevices beneath
the bear's eyes   O very sad and sweet
I'm standing in my kitchen   O honey
I'm staring at the honey bear's face.

ALONG THE STRAND

for Steve Levine

When I was a coke-dealer
I just snorted all the profits.
Or like the time I fell in love
with Morning, it was something
I could stay with. I would
stick around but it slipped
into noon and again I fell in love

   at twilight I was meditative
and prayerful and by night I
was truly in love with someone
I could not see.

The person who invented inventions
was the same one who
waited to see what everyone was
requesting and then she invented

inventing. I tasted that once
but now it is no longer new.

The countermen placing chairs atop
tables, the tables are clean
and the radio plays all the new
songs.

What night was it that you told me
how the last time you felt this
way you just walked and walked

well I am the ghost of the coffee
shops who started smoking
very late. My father told
me they cause cancer and
I still believe they cause
cancer.

There is something wonderful about
plastic tables that resemble wood
and I am dreaming of a tree
by a stream that resembles
plastic.

For I am inventing again.

And I am walking backwards.
I grow deeply religious
as a child and as a
well-adjusted nun I am grateful
to the child who grew
me.

I am grateful to Dad's tip-
off concerning cigarettes, and
believing in denouements your footsteps
have stopped—you are
gladly resting on your couch.

Vouching for the honesty of
morning, he left me, became
someone else who I found be-
neath a plastic tree at
noon. Vigorous twilight is
our resting place and

we will exchange glowing photos
in the night.

        Invention produces
pools and they are not in
demand.

I am endlessly walking and
a solid colored day is more
to my liking.

"You are my sunshine
my only sunshine"

      the singing voice
produces color, shades her
day. She is a nun of my
love who draws bands of
smoke which is prayer

I snorted all the profits. I
sleep on a pillow which is
my nose, I find it very
      religious.

my mother taught me sex was
dirty, which was exciting

she taught me love is romantic

I didn't start fucking till quite late.
Exciting, romantic,
I am quite sure it is the one
thing I have invented.

The times of the day, the ones
with names, they are the
stripes of sex unlike romance
who dreamlike is a continuous
walker,

obviously a solid colored day
is unexciting

I bring my best romance
to morning. I bring my best
romance to noon. Night

the old charmer is in love with
candles. Holds a fistful of
morning behind his back.

So you are no longer walking.
And this is no particular cigarette.
A beautiful nun may be dreaming
my life

       or I am inventing again.

In ancient greece a mystical
child examines three ribbons.

The oldest woman in this part of
town is aware of her hair.

Black white and grey. Even
as she lay dying. Even as
she first fucked and her lover's
words caressed her like smoke, inventing
pools in her gorgeous and tangled
black hair.

GREECE

This summer
I tell my friends
I intend to spend
a solid month
in Greece.

This is ridiculous
my friends say.
Look at yourself.
Your shoes are worn thin.
When rent time comes
you fall down on the street
and cry
until someone comes along
drops dollar bills on you.

I will go to Greece.
For a solid month.

Living on a Greek isle.
Bordered by the blue Aegean.
In a small stone house.
I can go to Greece
if I want.

On July 1st
sitting in my apartment
with my sandals on
I will be in Greece.

This is madness
my friends say.
You cannot travel by sheer
desire.
I agree with them. It's madness.
But in Greece I will be sane.

SKUPPY THE SAILOR DOG

I was just thinking about influential books in my life. Most of them were illustrated. I am thinking about one in particular, right now, unmootly titled "Skuppy the Sailor Dog." The plot was, or is, a little vague. Skuppy was a wandering sort of dog. Sailed the seven seas, made cameo appearances in various spots, one of which comes to mind is Turkey. Skuppy is standing in a sort of medina where he purchases a pair of purple slippers with curled up toes. How astonished I was at the thought of a dog inserting his paws in such shoes. Skuppy is never shown actually wearing the shoes.

They do appear in one scene in Skuppy's small mildly lit bunker. At this point in his life, it seems Skuppy is in ownership of his own small tug. He is lying on the lower bunk of a two-decker and is quite alone and somehow you feel he is alone on the entire boat, it is his boat.

Yet the lighting is alright. A single sailor's lantern hangs on the wall, a tawny cozy yellow sprays around the room in a warm twinkling. The purple shoes lie discreetly at the foot of his bunker, his striped sailor's shirt folded neatly on a single wooden chair.

He's asleep at this point, with an ever so slight smile coursing his mouth, more of a glow than a smile.

Having good dreams, other places, countries, infinite new shoes to buy and strange people to purchase from. It is night of course and the boat is softly at sea, moving on its own correct course. Storm-free and guided by Skuppy, smiling at his dreaming.

MEDIUM POEM

I was the second of three children.
Born in middlesex county. Smack
in the middle of the twentieth century.
I have no womb memories
to the point of doubting my tenancy.
After-life seems a dubious conjecture.
I'll tell you when I get there. Paus-
ing in the middle of ladders
I smoke a cigarette for Wednesdays
when I am comfortable. And it is always
Wednesday. And I am never
sure. And I am always here.

WELSH POETRY

Mainly it's the shape of the hills as the old soldier
    laments
Three blue cars rush by
In this, New York City, all of us are heroes!

Whose green eye is upon my tennis shoe
Three birds land upon my firescape O love
My bewilderment is blind, has no season.

Three dogs are barking from three blocks away
Cool August wind blows through my sly silver screen
The year is latening, Hush, hear the dogs again.

MY CHEAP LIFESTYLE

After a bourbon
I came in turned on the tube
Lit a joint and watched Monterey Pop
Nearly wept when Janis came on
Janis's legs kicking on stage was a memorable sight
Janis does her sweet little Texas girl smile as
her act finishes. She kicks her heels
And Otis Redding is so sexy.
Millions of young Americans experience religion for
        the firsttime
In their lives
Or so the cameras would inform us
I'm concerned about manipulation in this media
How one gains such wonderful power
But of course I'm too tired
Thrilled by the process of bringing down a familiar
        blanket
Upon my bed
It's nearly fall
Nearly winter
I expect the stars will be bright
The woods full of bears.

ON THE DEATH OF ROBERT LOWELL

O, I don't give a shit.
He was an old white-haired man
Insensate beyond belief and
Filled with much anxiety about his imagined
Pain. Not that I'd know
I hate fucking wasps.
The guy was a loon.
Signed up for Spring Semester at MacLeans
A really lush retreat among pines and
Hippy attendants. Ray Charles also
once rested there.
So did James Taylor . . .
The famous, as we know, are nuts.
Take Robert Lowell.
The old white-haired coot.
Fucking dead.

TEXAS

I'm nearly crying for it—
looking at the large coloured map on his wall
poor TEXAS looking big-as-life
and dying to secede
Mama, did Annie Oakley ever cry? Or,

Mother is it true she couldn't cry
that's why she could shoot so well?

O Mama,
I just want to cry
sitting here looking at TEXAS across
the face of the map

so big & so lonely
I just want to get a beebee gun
and shoot that fucking state to bits

Sappho's Boat

1982

JOAN

Today, May 30th, Joan
of Arc was burned.
She was 19 and
when she died
a man saw white doves
fly from her mouth.

Joan was born in 1412
between Lorraine
and Champagne. Joan
was raised on legends.
Merlin said France would be
lost by a woman and saved
by a virgin. Joan was
not an adventurous girl, not
a tomboy, but very dreamy,
good, stay-at-home,
the baby of the family.
Joan never got her period.

She heard these voices
in the bells, she saw angels
in colored glass. She believed
the sun moved around
the earth because that's
what she saw. She believed
God wanted Charles VII
to be King of France
because that's what Michael,
Catherine & Margaret told
her when she listened to
the bells. Her father
said he'd drown her

if she didn't stop this
nonsense.

She was 19 years old
when they burned her body in the middle of town
while she was still alive. A white dove
came out of her mouth as she died.
Five hundred and forty-eight years ago today.
A dove leaped right out of her mouth.

"ROMANTIC PAIN"

And in the first bar
the woman next to me said, "
How would you like to be introduced
to a couple of muscle-bound . . ."
Then she talked about when she
had been chef, "Moist juicy
salad with russian dressing"
I gulped my bourbon & walked
out the door.
The second bar was all women.
Bartender, a chubby Diane Keaton.
Woman to my left, also
in the bar business. Woman
to my right, passed out.
I sipped my bourbon and listened
         to the jukebox.

I'd been asleep all day. I wanted to
be tired again. I looked up
and the sky was very dark.
I must see morning. I must
get off my ass, walk
and get tired.

Passed Canal Street. Walked through the plaza
of the criminal courts. Lit a cigarette
near a potted tree on Chambers Street.
World Trade towers immense quiet and barely
lit. Past the giant post office,
patriotic trucks coming in and out of the garage.
Retreat to the womb. A pregnant silence.
Rounding the corner, catholic relief place,
free lunches for old sailors. I
decide to ride the escalator

like I never do . . . up into the
ferry building. A last resort.
People sacked out on wooden benches.
Strange ladies room with door
wide open so everyone watches you look at
yourself. No one watches.
All crashed out on benches. I re-assemble
a red-stained newspaper. Get askance
stares like I'm a young bag lady.
I looked pasty in the bathroom.
Eyes like raccoons. My hair's screwed up.
My jacket looks "boxy."

The sign that says NEXT BOAT
goes green. We herd on,
rumpled, tobacco-mouthed, the black guy
calling the white woman with the little dog
"Weird" "a weird bitch"
He looks to me. Looks at me.
I try to tell him it's OK,
I am a weird bitch. The boat smells of
donuts and is filled with cops,
conductors, strange people coming home
from strange nights. I go in the
ladies room & see the woman
with the little dog. She plucks a
Winston from her pack. And an
oriental woman. Terribly neat. I
want to look at myself in the mirror
but I look so shitty I don't want
to expose my third-rate vanity. The
other two of us light a cigarette.
Three women at different angles
smoking cigarettes. We each sneak

peeks at ourselves in the mirror.
Push this piece of hair. Move
that collar   Inspect that eyelash.
          I can see us from overhead
and call the configuration "Feminism"

And the boat pulls out. I am brave
I am Hart Crane, I push the
     brown door aside and stand out on
          the deck. This is what I
came here for. The "me" movie,
          me on the deck in slight rain at
          5 A.M. looking at the Statue of Liberty
swathed in mist. I want to wave.
I always want to wave at her.

It's kind of cold and I think of
          various deaths in my family,
          how I'd go to see various gravestones
trying to exert some sorrow. Trying to
          create the sorrowful setting as
this one is "romantic pain," me alone in the
          rain on a boat and it's cold
          and I want a cigarette.
I huddle under the overhanging upper deck
          trying to light one. A cop comes
          by & I stealthily turn,
the wind picks my pack from my hands
          and I chase it and it scares me
me running on this deck &
          I think how desperate I was
          looking and I think the
          cop thinks now that I'm
going to jump & I sit on the

orange boat-bench
thinking what a fucked up reason for
suicide that would be,
just living up to some cop's anticipation.
Ha! I chuckle,
my kind of death

and I head downstairs
where the scum are allowed to
smoke, the windows thick
with grime, the smell of
decades of sour-mouthed
smokers   and I smoke.
And I watch Staten Island
approach.

Feeling the fool
I make a U-turn in the
hallway & look for the entrance
to the New York ferry.

I hope the crew is different.
I check the name of the boat but
it doesn't matter. I didn't
notice the other boat's name.

I make my perfunctory
tour of the deck. I feel
like Hart Crane. The wind smacks my
hair, washes it over my cheeks &
I wish I could cry.
The boat feels right this time.

Downstairs to smoke.
I always smoke. And it's crowded
          this time. Morning people,
foggy like night people but cleaner.
          Clean shirts, nylons, heels
     people drinking coffee as they
     smoke their cigarettes. The
          fat man over there,
               he keeps winking at me.
     I think, thinking I have no subway
          money, "For 50 cents I'll
     give you something to wink
               at."

All the way home
          through Chinatown, through
          the Bowery, back in the
business section, the awakening city,
     sitting on the bench across
          the street from
     the brand new FAMILY COURT
          building,

     I keep looking for it, that wonderful
          10, the 20 dollar bill
          waiting for me, lying on the
ground. I keep my head
          down all the way home. My feet
          hurt. And I missed the
          dawn. The
     goddamn dawn, Said Hart Crane.

LA VITA NUOVA

Love is an assumption
that is my argument
rudely transposing me
as a certain process
or in relationship to sanity
or I suppose this is an argument
between the body &
the soul
whether the chicken hatches
the egg.
Alone in my soul
or through the bodies of others
which confuse
& disarm
in a really provocative manner.
O
what financial disaster
to lie among sheep
propose that all men are sheep
all women.
Plato has me hot in drag
and they're all brilliant
perceptions. Who amongst
me is really getting off? Trans-
positions rudely transposing me.
In my argument I am amused.
I'd really like to tell
you of my love. But
in describing I would name,
lose
my love in attempts
to praise.
You must know I'm talking to you.
The absolutely horrible
cotillion of my thoughts.
I like to get really stoned
and revise everything I've ever done
Leaning
against the refrigerator
thinking I would kill to be

in bed with you right
now.
I get up.
Turn down my hamburger, re-establishing
myself
into a reading at the
Gotham, a man next to me
comments, "It's amazing
how Irish Catholics
are so uncomfortable inside
of their bodies . . ."
I smile knowingly

Bernadette Devlin crossing
the border
I get up again to put cheese on
my burger
theorizing of poems based
on appetite, the time elapsed
proceeding on the multitudes
of varying angles
separate climes . . .
Am I not inside my life?
Is my life the many places I can be
alive in & not get nostalgic
about?
Is man alone in the Universe?
What about me? I'm
replacing a lightbulb
and thinking about you.
I'm a phoney. The illusion of love
is no substitute
for the actual
experience of being a carpenter
which I have never
ever considered being.

EXPLODING THE SPRING MYSTIQUE

Good Morning, World! Captain Eileen here
At her little morning desk
Dying to tell you at the crack of dawn
How dearly she hates it
How Spring truly sucks.

Here we have it outside my morning window
Birds twittering, buds newly greening on perky branches
          "Tweet," another fucking bird.

And I had to go through a whole night to get here.
That's the part that's really hard to swallow.
I had to lie awake for hours thinking of how I hate just about
Every man, woman and child who walks the face of this earth
Myself included, I find self-hate extremely motivating

I thought of everyone I've ever fucked or wanted to and
Thought how unrewarding it was. "Can't take it with you!"
Like they say.
I thought of the conversations I've had.
Nearly the mystery was unraveled in 1962.
Then in 64, 67, 72, 73 and 74. And those were the transcendent
Conversations. Not to mention the warm friendly variety, or
The pitiful confessional motif. Both of you
Pour out your sorrows and feel instantly better.
"And I thought I was fucked up!" each thinks.

I thought of my dreams of becoming a great poet & then I
        thought of
My poet friends who dream no differently. I thought of my
Poet friends and how they have no right to live within
The revolting egocentric realities uniquely expressed in
Syntax all their own and then they print their own poems
In their own little magazines.

Was it Marlon Brando who said, "Looking up the asshole
     of death."
Anyhow, by 35 most poets either can't do it anymore
Or have ruined their lives or the lives of others or have
Simply realized that all of it was a farce.
Suddenly struck at 35 by the genuinely mediocre fact of your
     life
Which previously stood as a backdrop to the cosmos or
     culture
And now . . . Har, Har, Middle-Aged Poet!
Joke's on you. Broke and not very good-looking.

Though I don't plan to stop at this moment.
Sure, I hate my friends and they hate me and there's no one
     around to
fuck except the ones who won't fuck me and they like to
     torture me
And I like it—my poems keep getting better and better.
But the fact is
If I am no longer a poet, then I will have to face being a
     useless and
Mediocre human being now, rather than when I'm 35, as is
     the norm
35 will be terrifying.
A) Unless dead or raving mad or abandoned with a large
     shopping bag
And a pint of Wild Irish Rose, I will be B) teaching a
     workshop
or C) penning a villanelle, as one poet puts it, or
D) just taking a shit and suddenly the joke will be swarming
     all
Around me, a nettle of fears and doubts, cold icy sweat,
     perhaps
I'll be standing on a stage reading a fucking sonnet and

Whomp! "Your life is meaningless! This is the last
   message!"

"What, What . . ." I'll mutter, swinging my arms around
   spastically
But I know what it means: "You blew it, Baby It was a joke."
So I go home to my lover (If I'm that fucking lucky when I'm
35 . . . Why should it start then? But listen, this is the clincher . . .)

I go home to my lover, who's of course in her early 20s
A Younger Poet. There's a note on my pillow
Sorry, Honey, you peaked.
Arrrgh! I shriek at the heavens.
All those years I chortled at men: Ha! you guys are done in
at 18. Your "prime." We women don't peak until 35.
I collapse on my bed, a sexual and artistic homicide.
Though still breathing, and it is Spring.

MY RAMPANT MUSE, FOR HER

Tuesday night   reading *For Love* on
my bed. Or writing *For Love*
    poem is wishing
      when I stop waiting. One thousand times

I've read & wrote *For Love*
      wear my sneakers, drink
my bourbon,
         be 28 in spite of me

      in mirrors, Christ!
     I look fucking *old*

        What does the evening
mean? I could fall for lamp-light,
    radio-song,
    "the oval shaped frame of which
he was particularly fond . . .

        For Love I would dream
when my schemes fall through, Man,
     could that little girl dance! *For Love* I will read
it 10,000 times   for my tomboy cousin Jean Marie,
     for radio song, *For Love*
I would not pity me, my 28, sneakers, bourbon
         the unseen
    future of my communications, and   the lamp-
    light, Her, she holds me here, so
    rampantly
     in her evening beauty.

WHAX 'N WAYNE

for Barbara

THE stars were glowing tonight
like all the paranoia in the universe

The air was chill
though it's early March
but that makes sense

Doesn't it, Love, Doesn't it?
and a five-dollar bill
is cold upon my ass, my blood is cold,
footsteps shattering the stairs
up to my level
then past it.
I only want a place on the line, I don't
want it to stop with me or start
with me, really I don't want it to know I'm here
at all, I only love what finds me invisible
and touches me deeply. Cold does that
and that's how I love the vanishing winter. I used to count
breaths in the night, one night I counted the church-bells
     falling
into a marsh and growing silent. It was two days before I dis-
covered boys, and tonight is two days after. I feel like
a woolen sock on the line, rippling, the season doesn't care
about me and I'm using it without its permission.
It's the new god, the one that doesn't know about me at all,
who misses me in movies, restaurants, who doesn't count my
wheels spinning—who could count silence? *that's the one I*
     love.
Loneliness sharpens into something sweeter, my sadnesses
     sharpening

themselves, christian thorns, You bet! Apples bananas
    particularness
which doesn't exist at all is a bird too big for churches so
churches grow as good as *movies, restaurants*   silence is
    running
tonight to get hot coffee, to smoke, to breathe
everyone is going home to someplace, me too, love creates
    loneliness,
I never knew that before.

Television is what the night eats.
I eat some soup, some bread, old black coffee reheated like
    favorite
shoes, you're like a fireplace I just want to be around.
Five bucks chill upon the ass, I think I'll buy the morning
    and some
of the afternoon. O pink tulip, *2 yellows,*
the length of this room, peaceful cats, outside it's cold,
damn it whatever happened to Spring? She comes before
    the other,
don't you know, you know, Primavera—*get it, get it*, get it?
I can stand in back of anyone I want, man or woman and
    anyone
who wants to stand in back of me is welcome, in fact they
    can stand in
front of me if they know how to do it, *do you get it?*
I think we are an army of trees. When I tripped
I only wanted to sit down everything was moving so much,
catholic poets only pray, no matter what they say
if I'm really vain I could propose to jump back into the pool,
just like it was a room, just like I'm not a stupid feather on
an immense wing, Love's taught me a loneliness I never
    imagined.
This side of the hallways, umm I don't know . . . smokier? I

always

thought I really loved Dante but now I know what he
    meant.

Mark says 9 represents chaos,

Dante thought 9 was the music of the spheres.

Mark is a musician and if you could draw a line between
    those two guys

I would call it history, hang a sock or two like me.

Affluence is holding out a dollar and receiving exactly what
    you want,

I call that economics, when I say "television" you know
    exactly

what I mean, I call that a modern idea, a word, "television,"

get it? Let's do it again: "time," Take the word breast,

take tit, what gets erotic is which word you prefer, what gets

warm is speechless . . . the cold things are easy to enumerate:

stars, paranoia, ideas under blankets

kiss my teeth. If a woman wakes up remembering her dreams

and she tells her lover and she doesn't lie at all

and the next day the lover dreams something entirely different

and all day both lovers think about each other's dreams

and go and have different dreams the next night

and they just enjoy telling the dreams each morning

with their coffee. If a cat nibbles on flowers

I lift it off the table and make it stop because it is ugly.

Dreams are some kind of flowers and when I pour coffee
    into my cup

this morning, for example, and I feed the cats this stuff I
    wouldn't

eat, I go to the bank, drink some orange juice at Binibon's.

Stuff with real pieces of orange in it. I drink a real big glass

of the stuff. The *New York Post* has one article about
    "peace,"

one about "terrorism." A guy in Weehawken is watching

The Ten Commandments on "television" *Boom*
a cuban storefront explodes while Moses is receiving the
     tablets.
Let's call that channel religion. Or science fiction.
Then the *New York Post* has an article about SHAPING UP.
I'm always thinking about that and I suppose my body
     reforms
accordingly. Lover, lover, here's a flower.
It doesn't think, It's like my mother.
I wasn't interested in the newspaper
it was just something I needed to hold. All the time I have
     dreams
that could have happened. "No more orange juice" or
     someone turns
to me and speaks a line I just wrote and I wonder if they
read a poem of mine lying on my desk or am I dreaming or,
I don't know, maybe there's different flowers in the vase
from when I fell asleep—well I don't live alone so there's no
reason to be surprised that different flowers are in the same vase.
When I dream I dream nothing extraordinary. That's what
     I'm
trying to say. If something's broken maybe the cat did it.
The wooden counter at Binibon's is more interesting
than the newspaper but if I sat here reading the counter
I'd look like an asshole. Reading a little bit
from each article I read like a bird.
I used to read like a horse until I went to college.
I felt all that knowledge coming at me through a screen.
Television fills the silence, I pay my check and leave a tip.
"The word is at the end; it's the thing's dead body." Words
of the Baby Bertolt Brecht. O—please pick up your grilled
tomato and cheese—please *eat* it. I didn't mean what I
said. All week long I've seen nothing but Lilacs.
Up and down Lexington Avenue, St. Mark's Place, through

windows of classy restaurants. But there's nothing
classy about lilacs; they used to line the trees on the street
where I lived. Children in spring bringing home big
armfuls, marching up twilit spring nights carrying
purple lilacs home to mothers waiting on screened porches.
Nineteenth century flower book says *Lilac*—Purple,
first emotions of love. Surprised me, I expected
death, something melancholic and fading. I am so taken
by these flowers these days. Days expanding and shrinking
so I am sure I am no form at all. Just your eyes and
my stupidity. Some people are so sure they aren't loved
they'll throw themselves to the task of being hateful. If
only I could buy some Lilacs on a full-moon night and run
here panting and wild. Be something perfect that doesn't
count and change. But I grew up where lilacs were free,
didn't everyone? So I'll just watch them all spring
in restaurants and flower shops . . . full and soft
as the lights go down, the moon comes up and another
season starts shouldering in. But the purple lilacs
are the most beautiful and I will always love you.

YELLOW TULIPS

I was walking along the sidewalk
in all the daily pain
& miserable faces & awful air.
Up above in a flower box
were yellow tulips, too real
to be real, so big
and sexual-looking in
that funny way flowers
always are. I guess
they were like heads
poking in from another
world. How do you
like Wednesday, you
beautiful things?

NEW YORK TULIPS

Then a group of you
found singing in a park
around a stupid old historical statue
Some tulips are completely
red, and some are terribly yellow.
Then the others shaded by both
maybe less clearly this or that.
But the mixed tulips
I love for their compassion.
They soften the blows
of this & that
I find them very beautiful.

LORNA & VICKI

Inside the White House lives the President
of the United States and the First Lady lives
with him. It makes me think about history:
amazing that anyone could,
or would want to live in there
especially to live with a guy who lives
in there. To live with some children, too.
Lesbian mums are shaking in the breeze
or to really tell the truth
this Smith-Corona is shaking the table
is shaking the grey stone mug that holds
the lavender mums so they shake.
I was riding down 5th Avenue yesterday and
the jostling vehicle started getting me off
and I started pressing my finger
against the seam of my jeans between my
legs—it got even better,
but then I thought "Oh Eileen, let nature
take its course. I've had orgasms sitting
at the back of the bus—on the far
left, right over the motor. And pedaling
up a hill on a hot summer day I was nearly knocked
off my bicycle by one but I was young
and thought it was a religious experience.
Masturbation will always be my favorite
form of sex, though if I was a tree
I'd just stand there in the breeze.

My mother used to spend a lot of her summer
evenings trying to cajole me
into doing the dishes. Eventually she'd do
this thing called "getting them started"—
or "letting them soak" I couldn't stand it.

Same way I can't stand this Smith-Corona
growling or humming while I'm looking for
a word. I like to do my waiting in silence—
I don't mind that pup yapping out my window
she's not even mindful of my mums
or my mother or you napping on the couch
or . . . Soaking dishes irritated my abandon.
Despite the fact I'm putting it off,
something's getting done. Each moment the job
gets a little easier and by the time
I slide my hands into the water and pull
out a plate: "Your idea was a good one, Mom.
Several hours of soaking have certainly loosened
up the food particles clinging to this evening's
dishes. I'm sure these'll be done in a jiff
thanks to you." Or water,
but that's the point. And sun is much the same.
If you put a couple of tea bags in a quart jar
of water and set the whole mess on your fire-escape
you wind up with something called Sun Tea.
Just think about it. Add some lemons.
It makes me wonder what wind can do—
while you're not even looking. Apparently
it jostles the leaves and petals too
--it's nature's favorite form of sex I bet. Turning
rain into a storm, knocking the angles of rain-
drops around like pool balls. Silently
though. Not the storm but the movement.
Movement is pretty quiet as long as it's not work.
I guess it was Thursday morning during a tropical
storm called David that I put on this tarp-type
poncho and went up on the roof
to see a lunar eclipse. Naturally the storm
had masked the event—the sun was a smudged

peach but loaded somehow—it actually felt magnetic.
The moon doing this thing you couldn't see,
well I was standing on my roof inside magic
a very mad and pleased Druidical woman
I wanted to pray to somebody or something,
wind or rain or downstairs in the warmth
when I took my clothes off and got
back in bed and fell asleep.

Not Me

1991

A POEM

It's a new year; you try to stick your keys in
the door. A neighbor's feet are coming down—
your fingers slip. His wrist goes for
the knob—because he's "in." That's the problem
with doors. The people inside have no patience
with my fumbling. What kind of year is this?
Life is a vow that frightens as it deepens.
You know which ones. I've never written a poem
to you before. Wearing my organs outside.
Or am I in? Lifting myself like a chalice to time.
A can of coke spinning on the floor.
You're right. I'm different. That might be all
we invented this year. In light of the mass
interpretations, translations, migrations . . .
in spite of all that it's great that we did
one single thing—to be different.
And now *that it shows* we should go really slow.
Wearing our difference like streamers or leaves
bringing our gifts to the city. To watch the
monster unwrap us. Naked and forlorn.
And I'm not like anyone else. Feeling my
foot I hear music. Bridging the city.
It's not the poor, it's not the rich, it's us.
And improved public transportation. And cable TV.
I'm giving up the idea of writing a great poem.
I hate this shitty little place. And a dog takes
a bite of the night. We realize the city was
sold in 1978. But we were asleep. We woke
and the victors were all around us, criticizing
our pull-chain lights. And we began to pray.
Oh God, take care of this city. And take care
of me. Cigarettes and coffee were always enough
in my youth. Now when I wake up thousands
of times in the day. I was in the process

of buying my love a shepherd's flute. And a thin
hand picked the one wanted off the top of the
pile. The one I heard which played so sweet.
And I bought a dud. Hardly better than
a soda bottle. Swell, you said. Well the back-pack
you gave me has started to rip. And the scarf,
well I love the scarf but I keep re-living
that Canal Jean remark. Cause there's no place
for the ironic in plain living. It goes too
fast so you must be direct. Symbolically
I want my black jersey back. Realistically
you must give it to me because I will keep
talking to your machine if you don't.
Our mayor is a murderer, our president
is a killer, Jean Harris is still not
free which leads me to question the
ethics of our governor who I thought
was good. There is an argument
for poetry being deep but I am not that argument.
There is an argument which chiefly has to do
with judging things which have nothing
to do with money as worthless
because you don't make any money from them.
Did you call your mother a fool when
she gave you your oatmeal in the morning.
I cannot explain my life from the point of
view of all the nooks and crannies
I occupied in my childhood yet
there I sat, smoking. More than anything
I want privacy. If I keep doing this
you will leave me alone. And what about
poor children. Dying in the street
in Calcutta today. Or little swollen
bellies in Africa. A public death

of course has no song. At some point
I decided I would want to die
in my home. And so I would have
to have it, as others would
have to have none. Sometime
after they sold New York
I began seeing you. I was dreaming
but I felt your judgment, and I saw
your face. And a woman stepped out of my
house and she opened the door.

EDWARD THE CONFESSOR

I have a confession to make
I wish there were
some role in society
I could fulfill
I could be a confessor

I have a confession to make

I have this way when I step
into the bakery on 2nd Ave.
of wanting to be the only
really nice person in the store
so the harried sales woman
with several toned hair
will like me. I do this in all
kinds of stores, coffee shops
xerox shops, everywhere I go.
And invariably I leave my keys,
xeroxing, my coffee
from the last place
I am being so nice. I try
so hard to make a great
impression on these neutral
strangers right down to
the perfect warm smile
I get entirely lost and
stagger back out onto
the street, bereft
of something major.
It's really leaning
too hard on the everyday.
My mother was
the kind of woman who
dragging us into stores

always seemed to charm the pants
off the cashier. She was such
a great person, so human
though at home she was
such a bitch, I mean really
distant. I imitate her and
I don't do it well. She didn't
leave her wallet
or us in a store.
I'm just a pale imitation
it is simply not my style
to open the hearts of
strangers to my true
personhood. I hope you accept
this tiny confession of what
I am currently going through.
And if you are experiencing
something of a similar nature
tell someone, *not me*,
but tell someone. It's the new
human program to be in. It would
be nice for at least
these final moments if
we could sigh
with the relief
of being in
the same program
with all the
other humans
whispering
in school. I can't quite locate
the terror, but I am trying
to be my mother
or Edward the Confessor

smiling down on you with up-praying
hands. I am looking down at the
tips of my boots as I step
across the balcony of the
church excited to be allowed
to say these things. Outside my church
is a relationship. On 11th street
this guy and this woman are selling
the woman so they can
get more dope. All their things
are there, rags and loaves of
bread and make-up.
And there was—
this was incredible.
Two men lying by the door
of the church giving
each other blow-jobs.
They were sort of street
guys, one black one white.
I said hey you can't do
that here. They jumped
up, one spit come

out of his mouth. If you don't
get out of here I'll call
the cops. Don't call the
cops we'll go, we'll leave.

That was a shock. That was more
than I expected to see in
a day. Something about
seeing the guy spit
come out of his
mouth. He didn't

have to do that.
I guess I scared
him. I couldn't
believe my eyes.
I was scared too.

HOLES

Once when I passed East Fourth Street off First Avenue,
I think it was in early fall, and I had a small hole
in the shoulder of my white shirt, and another on
the back—I looked just beautiful. There was a
whole moment in the 70s when it was beautiful
to have holes in your shirts and sweaters.
By now it was 1981, but I carried that 70s style
around like a torch. There was a whole way of
feeling about yourself that was more European
than American, unless it was American around
1910 when it was beautiful to be a strong
starving immigrant who believed so much
in herself and she was part of a movement
as big as history and it explained the
hole in her shirt. It's the beginning
of summer tonight and every season has
cracks through which winter
or fall might leak out. The most perfect
flavor of it, oddly in June. Oh remember
when I was an immigrant. I took a black
beauty and got up from the pile of poems
around my knees and just had too much
energy for thought and walked over to
your house where there was continuous
beer. Finally we were just drinking
Rheingold, a hell of a beer. At the
door I mentioned I had a crush on both
of you, what you say to a couple. By
now the kids were in bed. I can't
even say clearly now that I wanted
the woman, though it seemed to be
the driving principle then, wanting
one of everything. I was part of
a generation of people who went to

the bars on 7th street and drank the
cheap whiskey and the ale on tap and dreamed
about when I would get you alone. Those
big breasts. I carried slim notebooks which only
permitted two or three-word lines. I need you.
"Nearing the Horse." There was blood in all my
titles, and milk. I had two bright blue pills
in my pocket. I loved you so much. It was
the last young thing I ever did, the end of
my renaissance, an immigration into my
dream world which even my grandparents
had not dared to live, being prisoners
of schizophrenia and alcohol, though
I was lovers with the two. The beauty
of the story is that it happened.
It was the last thing that happened
in New York. Everything else happened
while I was stopping it from happening.
Everything else had a life of
its own. I don't think I owe
them an apology, though at least
one of their kids hates my guts.
She can eat my guts for all
I care. I had a small hole in
the front of my black sleeveless
sweater. It was just something
that happened. It got larger
and larger. I liked to put
my finger in it. In the month
of December I couldn't get
out of bed. I kept waking
up at 6 P.M. and it was Christmas
or New Year's and I had to
start drinking & eating. I remember

you handing me the most beautiful
red plate of pasta. It was like your cunt
on a plate. I met people in your house
even found people to go out and fuck,
regrettably, not knowing about
the forbidden fruit. I forget
what the only sin is. Somebody
told me recently. I have so
many holes in my memory. Between
me and the things I'm separated
from. I pick up a book and
another book and memory
and separation seem to
be all anyone writes
about. Or all they
seem to let me read.
But I remember those
beautiful holes on
my back like a
beautiful cloak
of feeling.

APRIL NOON

What's the two best smelling
things in the world?
The inside of my brief-
case
and then this
person
I know. The birds
are screeching
for attention
today. Wind blowing
boats down the
street. People in
leather back-
packs talking
about Chanel,
my laundry *Plump*
in my hand.
I can see you through
the grid of
my life. A slight
distance, doing
your things.
I want to go
take your temperature
go to Russia
with you.
Look in your
eyes, so
foreign
& blue. They look
like a couple of question
marks. I stand with
my cup in my
hand, this
day, while
it's waiting
for You.

THE SADNESS OF LEAVING

Everything's
    so far away—
my jacket's
    over there. I'm terrified
    to go & you
won't miss me
    I'm terrified by the
bright blues of
    the subway
    other days I'm
    so happy &
prepared to believe
    that everyone walking
down the street is
    someone I know.
The oldness of Macy's
    impresses me. The
    wooden escalators
    as you get
higher up to the furniture,
    credit, lampshades—
    You shopped here
    as a kid. Oh,
    you deserve me! In
    a movie called
        Close Up—once in
a while the wiggly
bars, notice
  the wiggly blue
    bars of
    subway entrances,
the grainy beauty,
    the smudge. I won't
kill myself today. It's

too beautiful. My heart
    breaking down 23rd
St. To share this
    with you, the
    sweetness of the
        frame. My body
    in perfect shape
        for nothing but
        death. I want
    to show you this.
    On St. Mark's Place
        a madman screams:
    my footsteps, the
        drumbeats of Armageddon.
        Oh yes bring me
        closer to you Lord.
    I want to die
        Close Up. A handful
    of bouncing yellow
        tulips for David.   I
        admit I love tulips
            because they
        die so beautifully.
    see salvation in
    their hanging heads.
A beautiful exit. How do
        they get to feel so free? I am
    trapped by love—
        over French fries
        my eyes wander to
            The Hue Bar. A blue
        sign. Across the
    life. On my way to
        making a point,

to making logic, to not
falling in love to-
night and
let my pain remain
unwrapped—to push
the machine—Paul's
staying in touch, but
oh remember Jessica
Lange, she looked so
beautiful all
doped up, on her
way to meet King
Kong. I sit
on my little red
couch in February
how do they get
to feel so free
1,000,000 women
not me moving through
the street tonight
of this filmy
city & I
crown myself
again & again
and there
can't be
two kings.

HOT NIGHT

Hot night, wet night
you've seen me before.
When the streets are
drenched and shimmering
with themself, the
mangy souls that wan-
der & fascinate its
puddles, piles of
trash. Impersonal
street is a lover
to me—growling
thunder   lightning
to flash and light
up 7th as a little
mangy boy weaves
towards me &
laughing couples
kiss the puddles
with intended
sex in bright
shirts. It could
be another city
but it's this
city where
I start
being alone
& alive bringing
my candles
in while
I go walking
in the rain.
I think I
need a bowie

knife, a
pistol, a squealing
horn. You've
seen me before
hardly ever as
charged up as
now at the
end of my
rope by a
window in
the rain. July
is full of
pleasance, things
that can be
pushed to
fill to the
end of
the summer where
no one's ever
surprised to
have made it
to September
when something
lives—the
culture made
inside. In July
I am filled
with the death
of the streets,
you've seen
me before—
you're a wit-
ness to the
death of

my innocence
which came
teetering here
without ap-
petite. If
anything lives
I have seen
it in the streets & why
am I falling in love
now with the old
& the scabrous. Why
am I giving my money away. Sunday
I photographed mounds
of trash, finally
turned the focus on
me, a portrait I
could accept. I
feel erotic, oddly
magnetic to the
death of things
emptily attracted
to the available
empty space,
a step, or
I will not tell
you where I've
been but I
do & do not
belong. When the
dawn begins
I'm blue & lonesome
give me twilight
then the night,
let me be lost

in the lonesome
place, the human
sea of no one.
Drivel passes from
the mouths of
babes, smart shirts
bopping along,
art faces california
faces, the proud
march of culture
in New York City
Man are we buzzed
the screaming pork-
chops on the 4th
of July, the
disintegration of
the Hell's Angels,
can be loved,
now there are
10, can be
inclusive now
I smell death
everywhere. I hardly
think it's in me though
it always has been
my baby blossom,
I hope I make
it through the night
unplanned, nothing
dazzles me now,
who's driving? God?
I don't believe in
God. New notebook
I'm scared. My

hand tries to fly
free, but it's my
life, not my
death. Make
an inventory of
your occupations
remember now
there is sugar
in your coffee
and the band
will catch
you if you
fall. Remember,
remember—what
were Hart Crane's
last words—you
read them in
the Strand. My
dear—I've simply
disgraced myself.
You know a
genius when you've
seen one, don't
you, I'm one.
Take a good look,
you've seen me
before. Don't
turn back. Isn't
it a famous image
of the end of
Love, the famous
ride on the ferry.
Departing from
Land the Love, the

famous prow parting
the water now
as I jab my hand
inside you now
and churn. My bike
falls apart. The chain
collapses, the brakes
stuck, the wheel
wiggles, taking in-
ventory of my
teeth if they do
not look like
they will make
the long haul
I will leave
with them. My
poetry is here
for the haul,
the lonely woman's
tool—we have
tools now, we
have words &
lists, we have
real tears now,
absence, rage &
missing you is
not possible in
the New York
rain because
your name
is caught between
the drops &
I might throw
up, I can't

because it is
not beautiful
& I'm a
ward of the
state. Silly
children in
hats, raving
junkies, so
what, discreet
children, bad
songs, where's
the art? My
drivel in
the rain, or
the la-la-
the tape. I have
no hope for
my culture now.
It prefers fictions
over journals, it
doesn't want
my lives so
I choose streets
like a billionaire,
prove my coffee
counts. I
pick up "you" like
my midnight
rattle I shake
at the devil
of the night
that does not
scare me. It's
true I've done

nothing right
but I'm driven
by the rainbows
of trash in
puddles, the
frames posters,
& windows, the
marked sidewalks,
stray shoes,
can you imagine
selling used magazines,
poetry books on
a blanket, click,
dividing my time
by the tables, the
walks, 27, going
oh, oh, what
pain I need
whiskey sex
and I get
it.

AND THEN THE WEATHER ARRIVES

I don't know no one
anymore who's
up all night.
Wouldn't it be fun
to hear someone
really tired
come walking
up your stairs
and knock on your door.
Come here
and share the rain
with me. You.
Isn't it wonderful to hear
the universe
shudder. How old it all,
everything,
must be.

How slow it goes, steaming
coffee, marvelous morning,
the tiniest hairs
on the trees' arms
coming visible.

I like it better,
no one knows

sweetness, moving your
lips in silence.
Closing your eyes all night.

It's so much better
disarming myself
from terror, and light

passing through
a painting I stuck
on a window
earlier, when I was scared.

It's great, it's really great.
Trees hold the world
and the weather
moves slow.

Even a body dissolves
and takes a place, incorrectly,
everywhere I would
like to nuzzle,
and plants a heart
in the world
voiceless.

I began knocking.
Ridiculous. Just to hear
your echo back,
arm against face

just to stop those fucking
trucks, my thoughts
of vanishing
into that sweetness.

NOVEMBER

Because I'm sure that nothing lasts
I have to be very sure where I am
I can hear the dripping of the faucet
and the cries of little birds outside
and I have to be very sure that I love
because I'll never live like this again
and I'm sure that I love

I'm sure I'm closing in on something
the building isn't making that angle
of light for me. But I can see it.
It silences the cat but it doesn't silence
me. That's why I let the cat be
around. My landlord doesn't think
my way. I couldn't be like that.
I'm sure that I love.

Obviously my heart lies clenched
in my fists. I must be thinking or
feeling this way. This poem's bad.
It wants to think or tell about
how it's felt. But it just seems
to beat along between punches
and silence.

I have to be very sure where I am.
I'm telling you so. If it weren't
for telling I'd be left with the plumbing
and birds, where I am, but I'm telling
you so.

I thoroughly respect the birds
because they're not even listening.
I do. I like them a lot.
For their poverty and lack of thought.
I love myself for my love, a dubious
gift, and I guess I need those
fucking pipes. Simplicity,
that's that. I guess I love you

and I need you, love telling you that
I have to be very sure where I am.

Listening and waiting.
I wish you'd call and tell
me something, my landlord wants
to know where I'm at, but
I'm telling you that nothing
lasts, it doesn't silence me
but it silences the cat
I have to be very sure where I am.

NEW ENGLAND WIND

Remember me this summer
under the eaves again
stretched out against
the sky again
like Orion's moon

when a breeze crawls
down a screen, pip, zing
or is that a cat
crawling up

Oh was I alone in the
first room I ever
had or who would've
writ this then? Me too
when I am mad.

O leave me alone with
my aching head,
panicky panicky
no where to go
pretty north & silly

the other night
under the eaves
in a rain at 4 o'clock
I woke up it was
so sexy, listened so
careful in the world
the next day
for who also heard it
dreamy-eyed, who could've
come up or I come down
for once from
the sky
to be what
fell.

MAD PEPPER

I wonder if anything really needs to be revived.
MAD magazine should probably be dead by 1984
rather than: $2.50 CHEAP. It's difficult
to impossible to just buy pepper. You
can get a vast amount on sale for $2.99
an exquisite amount for $1.49—nicely packaged
like a spice but it's just pepper. The tall
waiter leans over and says: Would you like
some freshly ground pepper on your salad?
Oh yes. Leaning over to my companion—
Oh, this is nice. Dan recommends I go
to MeadowSweet and get some special Lesbian
Pepper. Pepper's male I snort. I want
some cheap male pepper. *The Village Voice*
made me miserable, that damp skuzzy paper
those endless articles I should really
read and when I do I know less, wasted
a night or a morning. I boldly returned
and exchanged the *Voice* for *MAD* '84,
at least it's a pleasure owning that
silly gloss and will be entertained
at least once thinking: *MAD*'s not the same
as it used to be. Tennis anyone? The
margin was the best. Why don't women
have back-room bars. It just wouldn't
work, that's why. Pepper's male,
sea salt's female, it takes longer
to gather, waiting for the ocean
to dry up and come back, overwhelmed by
the immensity of it. It's nice to have
a friend like you to sit on the shore
with. Maybe I'll bring some pepper.
From MeadowSweet. I seek adventure
today. Wound up in a hardware

store, a meeting, superette &
a bodega looking for pepper. First
today I craved cheese, then (now) I crave
fish, some sushi to go, it's cheaper,
quick, broke again but I got my tools:
Spackle pan, roller, Scotch-brite pads
Ajax, all strong names, I look strong.
I must be strong. I bought Lotto,
I left early thinking I would meet
the thing in the street, I met Leonard
bumped into Tom in the coffee shop, that
was the thought, got confused in a
hardware store, the help look junked
out, I had to pee, walked back to
the coffee shop, asked for the
key, but the door was open. Oh, yes,
I got my hair cut today on Astor
Place, near the mall, where the pathetic
belongings of all are sold. Again &
again. Poverty's an ocean. I bought
a pen, a red one, reddish orange.
What do you think of the Lower East Side
Art Scene. Oh I don't know I guess
it's great. I mean I'm not connected,
I just bumped into a guy I know is
successful. He says he's trying to
not let it affect him, but still
I wondered if I said the right thing.
I think it's nice the neighborhood
looks different so I don't have to
move and my apartment's worth more.
So now I have to paint it because
the face is depressing, the face
of poverty. You said it's female

didn't you? That the face of poverty
is female which is a good line, it sounds
like a good line, but it takes more than
sound to make a good line. That's a good line.
It sounds true, doesn't it? A good
line sounds true.

Pepper's male is a good line.
But that's because it sounds
more like a place, Pepper's Mail.
I live in Pepper's Mail, New Jersey,
it distorts. It looks like it's going to rain.
Big things probably sound small at first.
Someone asks you for something and it
sounds really unimportant: Give me some
poems, I'd like to translate them into
Serbo-Croatian. Sure. Hound me, Bitch.
Later you get a post-card from Beograd
& you realize she wasn't kidding.
There could be a statue of me in the City Square
by now. Next time someone says pass me the
pepper, give it to them fast. I'm shy about
asking for things. I could sit at the table
dying but I can't get the necessary eye con-
tact from over there to ask for the butter.
I start saying, well you don't really need
it. That's right, pushing my beans around
merrily passing everything even my fork
to anyone who looks up in a flash. The strongest
things I know . . . humidity, fire-crackers, hunger,
the capacity of trees to grow leaves, it's what
I see when I'm looking around, I miss you so
much, but you are not the strongest thing
right now but what I see. Against a brick wall

a woman with one of the most beautiful bodies
I have ever seen drapes herself against three
dark sisters who carry her apparently in
something called *Bewegungsstudie*. <u>Motion</u> <u>Study</u>
my dictionary *übersetz*. I won't even tell you
what I thought, Pepperhead. Thursday, August
2nd. Some part of me is always quietly counting.
I think that is a good line. Stooges Anonymous.
Beverly Ipswich Rockport. A train schedule
I carried when I got on the wrong train.

The red light continues to blink on my answering
machine and I stepped out ages ago to pick
up a coke and some pepper, some cigarettes
Handy-wipes, I love them, and everything changed
it will never come back that clear single in-
tention, though it seems there were two or three.

THE SAD PART IS

I love the guy in the Laundromat
the way he hands things to me,
smiling, a nice pink slip
with a black number on
it. I've just handed
all my clothes over
to him, they're quickly
weighed, priced, he writes
the price down on the
slip and it's okay,
he smiles, I smile,
I walk out. It's funny
how I sit in this, the
inner sanctum of my
apartment with
the stove, the refrigerator,
overhead light. Down
there in the dark by
the window I've
got a desk but I like
it over here—it seems
warmer though the
radiator's down
there—I live
in a small place
and when I'm alone
I make it smaller
prefer it this
way, keep the action
in a small bright
place, wonder
where I'm going
but tonight
I've got
this light.

TRIANGLES OF POWER

Got a slice
burned the roof
of my mouth.
Knew I would
it was
delicious.

I fast-walked
someplace. My feet
were cold
but the
slice built
a fire
in my stomach.
I said
Thank you
to the
natural
elements:
cold night
digestion.

What is
it about
the January
feeling—
past everything
else, low-glowing
hunger that
propels me
around
I may be wrong,
predictable
to picture you

around here
or us over
there, it's a
miracle,
rolling golden
in the coldest
month looking
forward &
back from
so much
else, there
wasn't even
a noun around
I walked
in from
the snow
nearing Christmas
& you touched
my black
coat
with your
handsome
hand &
believe me
I came
lit. (&
am changed.)

PEANUT BUTTER

I am always hungry
& wanting to have
sex. That is a fact.
If you get right
down to it the new
unprocessed peanut
butter is no damn
good & you should
buy it in a jar as
always in the
largest supermarket
you know. And
I am an enemy
of change, as
you know. All
the things I
embrace as new
are in
fact old things,
re-released: swimming,
the sensation of
being dirty in
body and mind
summer as a
time to do
nothing and make
no money. Prayer
as a last re-
sort. Pleasure
as a means,
and then a
means again
with no ends
in sight. I am
absolutely in opposition

to all kinds of
goals. I have
no desire to know
where this, anything
is getting me.
When the water
boils I get
a cup of tea.
Accidentally I
read all the
works of Proust.
It was summer
I was there
so was he. I
write because
I would like
to be used for
years after
my death. Not
only my body
will be compost
but the thoughts
I left during
my life. I was
a woman with
hazel eyes. Out
the window
is a crooked
silo. Parts
of your
body I think
of as stripes
which I have
learned to
love along. We

swim naked
in ponds &
I write be-
hind your
back. My thoughts
about you are
not exactly
forbidden, but
exalted because
they are useless,
not intended
to get you
because I have
you & you love
me. It's more
like a playground
where I play
with my reflection
of you until
you come back
and into the
real you I
get to sink
my teeth. With
you I know how
to relax. &
so I work
behind your
back. Which
is lovely.
Nature
is out of control
you tell me &
that's what's so
good about

it. I'm immoderately
in love with you,
knocked out by
all your new
white hair

why shouldn't
something
I have always
known be the
very best there
is. I love
you from my
childhood,
starting back
there when
one day was
just like the
rest, random
growth and
breezes, constant
love, a sand-
wich in the
middle of
day,
a tiny step
in the vastly
conventional
path of
the Sun. I
squint. I
wink. I
take the
ride.

THE REAL DRIVE

My great sacrifice exists
between the inarticulate
fingers of a tree sparkling
up through a brooding blue
as I whale it to the gym
in a cab though the air
is wet tonight and I want
to take you in my arms
and go to Europe.

O baby we must. Kissing
all the droplets off your
back in the shower now
and the radiator's sizzling
against the loss and the
apparent despair and decay
in the walls of the way
I live. Anyone can see
it now, even Joan.
I can't change a thing
but it's warm, terrifically
warm against the oncoming
winter of 1986 when I was
born with you who are
always moving your teepee
away, but I usually follow.

I don't want to brow-beat
you, O black and white, black
and white. The cops in the
city whooping down First
like big dogs. I have to
stay true on the street
I was born on, this is

an oath, don't lie.
I am slipping, I am lying.

My great sacrifice exists
because everyone sees it
and I need that a lot.
I am such a big lesbian
that I have to jump
off a cliff. I am such
a handsome poet I have to
become an advocate of
verse and stop lying
and get rich.

Everytime I dress
better pretty soon
I'm speechless or
broke soon I hope.
O release me from
the hostage
of Oh, working for
you baby or what?

In the cab driving
through a slick woman's
arms I could've cried
because I was not
slipping and sliding
alone. It was you
in a beautiful dress
black and white,
black and white
I have felt things here
which I assumed belonged

to fourteen when I
was perfect, oh you
a man or something

wonderful.

The great sacrifice is—

she slides an icicle
down my blouse
she is a jerk

the wonder of the universe
is   She did not get spoilt

She can hold me
I can hold her
also.

Every bit of ice breaks
up. It flows down the
river streaming.

Tiniest glistening
droplets on the
branches of the
tree this winter

and the dampness
on your hair
in the light

when I go this
way and you
got your

coat, black,
wrapped

around you now
as you walk
home

with the street-lights

on your back

because you
are the

North.

AUTUMN IN NEW YORK

It's something like returning to
sanity but returning
to something I have
never known like
a passionate leaf
turning green
August almost gone
"—that's my name,
don't wear it out."
As if I doffed
my hat & found
a head or
had an idea
that was always
mine
but just came
home, the balloons
are going by so
fast. I lean on
buttons accidentally
jam the works
of what works
when I simply
am this
green.

MAL MAISON

And so I got some marigolds
instead of slitting
my wrists tonight.
And guess what I
had to live through
today—hanging on
to the phone with
my desperate wrist
on Sunday, guess
what I had to
live through, what
new shame, humiliation
rejection which I guess
it is, right, I could be
dead, right—and this
is so much better.
The smell of meat
cooking in the kitchen,
what could be worse,
I know what could
be worse—I could be
pregnant with you!
That's as bad as things
could be. I could be
having you, rather
than having a hamburger.
I could be getting
fucked in the ass &
whipped, going out
to a party or just
eating potato chips.
To count on anyone
is really stupid.
Especially big groups of

them. Glad to be here,
glad to stop you in
your tracks with
their incredible
lack of vision, their
way of continuously
making the future
impossible. I'm
left waking up,
running miles further
than anyone ever had
to before. Thinking
of those bloody stupid
bastards, each one
and their lack of
vision of how great
it could be, I'm not
having you, or having
them or having any
of it. I'm a remarkably
spiritual creature,
I am. Lifting my little
bow & arrow, poignantly
requesting guidance
from the trees or
my feet, or continuous
coffee. It's not con-
tinuous coffee, or
endless. What kind of
coffee is it that
will get me out of
corners, make me move
& keep talking to
people. Look at me

like an arrow on
my bike, whizzing
by like visiting
you. Pouring down
St. Mark's Place,
Quakers, angels
& drunks,
that's all I
see. Lots of
new puppies—
they're in season.

Failure, of course,
is a more interesting
obstacle than
joy. It makes me
stronger, right?
It makes me more
like Winston Churchill than
the normal
celebrity of
things going
well, procrastinating
& visiting, basking
in my latest vic-
tory about my-
self. What kind
of coffee? Invisible,
bottomless (like Sunday)
and religion. What
kind of coffee?
I'm going running
right now and see

if I can think
of that word.

The enormity
in my chest is
not depression
and I stopped
smoking, started
drooling six
weeks
back, I could
blame everything
on that, even
how close I
am to getting
a puppy, those
kind of feelings.
Mixed with this
intolerable sad-
ness I am learning
to tolerate. I imagine
all the big beautiful
clipper ships sailing
off to sea on a per-
fect blue day and
I am not on them.
You stand on the
dock & wave. That's
what they said to
me as they were
pulling up
the plank.
Yeah, why don't

you try it, wiping
a large sensitive
tear from my eye,
returning to the
town to have
breakfast &
get laid.

Oh, Love, I love
you so much. The crying
babies of the sirens
pass through the
town, I am expected
to do more &
more & more.

I learned
I could leave,
I felt I might
get caught or
else humiliate
myself by
being so
bad, doddering
look at this
autumn acting
like summer,
the world
giving Eileen
a checking
account &
not expecting
her to act
up. How

will I know
in this ball
of yarn if
I am acting
or feeling
correctly.

I'm really
depressed.
The best revolutionaries
like to give up on
hot nights in fall
and ponder how
they really have always
felt like
Joan of Arc
that is
if they
were awake.
And now
I have
a girlfriend
who is really
a cowboy &
now I have
embarrassed
her & really
lost her
again. And now
I am in an orange
dress with this
wild fringe at
a dark party
with big

white lamps
& there she
is! Oh you're
here, you're
here, you're
here. Coming
around the
corner to
where I
work, a large
old church
surrounded
by big iron
fence, a gate
and I'm memorizing
in a movie script
my other life . . .

OK, I'm this
woman, about
35—she's
been somewhere
else but now
she's here,
in a car, an unimportant
American one, maybe
blue-grey. And she
drives around Michigan,
maybe New Mexico,
Arizona, selling,
God, I don't
know what she
sells but she's
me and I know

all about her
life, how
she sells these
things out of her
car. I don't
really picture
her staying
some place,
her name is Margaret,
I like that. She
may have been
married, had
a kid (or two)
but she left
it for this
dreaming life—
where half-
bored she
roams the plains
of America,
and the painted
desert & the mediocre
cities of Illinois,
etc. She's just
moving her lips
very softly
I am not connected,
I am not connected,
very softly, laughing
very softly occasionally
oh, I am connected
to everything,
winks into the
rear view mirror

at her beautiful
bland sardonic
self, this American
woman, endlessly
riding like
an astronaut
inside the
land, she winks
and pops on
the radio,
hey—What's
that—Sarah
Vaughn singing
Autumn in
New York,
New York, hmmm,
that's funny.
Clicks the radio
off still
smiling, pops
a velamint
into her
mouth. This must
be shot very
close, the
woman's face
is the star,
not her
mind,
her face
is the
star
of that.
The brooding

lips in
America
looking
at the land-
scape
change.
The music
in America,
that junky
scratchy
music on the car
radio, the
endless miles,
all the bad
places to
eat—greasy,
meaty, tons
of men—you'd
think it was
their country,
the baseball
fields, the locker rooms,
war monuments, clubs,
bars, the highways,
the police department,
it's strangely
sinister to
this woman,
and she's wondering
about that.
As she's driving
around this big
sad, fabulous
country. A country's

like a flower
pressed in time,
she laughs
alone. And I'm
in love, all
by myself
for once,
my heart
is a radio,
I just want
to say that
I love you,
and we
have a lot
of *time*. She kisses
another & leaves
again. We are always
leaving, it is
so wrenching
like Autumn
in New York,
my way of loving
you is season
change each
departure
falls through
the air,
it may be
final, frightening
to be part
of something
immense
the world
going through

a change of heart,
my love for
you, utterly
willing to
be this
woman's face
the wandering
star of the
American mind,
her radio
is in my
heart, I
beg to
be there,
drifting
through
your changes
with you.
Each facial
expression
shifts, the
car wheel
turns as
a leaf
falls
in New York.
I love you,
I love you,
I love you,
. . . I would
never stop

if I was that
woman, but

I am. You
are too,
she's you,
Margaret,
Magda,
woman with the
Letter 'm'
for some
reason.
Perhaps
the Indians
know. Ask
my mother.

Momma, it's
cocktail
hour. The
time is
still
in the teens,
8:18, 8:19
& so forth.
I get separation
anxiety every
time the num-
bers achieve
a new cycle.
the 20s, the
30s. Here
goes the
hour, oops,
there is
another
one coming,

there is,
there is,
there cer-
tainly
is. I'm
drinking
an awful
lot of o-
range
juice, aren't
I? It's very
over-rated.
What is?
Oh . . . he puffed
smoke thoughtfully
into the horizon
. . . a lot of
things. Let's
use some
German words
& stuff.
Unterstehen—
be subordinate
to. Another,
gimme another
good German
word. They're
all tough
like that
aren't they?
Untergang.
I am a shipwreck.
I am a hungry
shipwreck.

I like this
German. Let's
keep going.
Fensterflügel.
In the case-
ment I saw
you. It was
the best. You
were framed
(like art)
yet I was looking
down on you.
(Like I like.)
I wonder if I can
go a little further
now. I left
". . . and I love
you" on some-
one's machine
today. No response.
I guess she was
just being ac-
cepting. Here is
the finest low-priced
German–English, English–
German dictionary
ever published.
Here on my desk.
Cover design
by Charles Skaggs.
Someone probably
one of you
knows. Charles.
Akzept. acceptance.

Ich habe Akzept. In
German (*auf Deutsch*)
all the nouns are
capitalized which
I think is powerful.
Swift little verbs
pushing the big
nouns around
the language.

AN AMERICAN POEM

I was born in Boston in
1949. I never wanted
this fact to be known, in
fact I've spent the better
half of my adult life
trying to sweep my early
years under the carpet
and have a life that
was clearly just mine
and independent of
the historic fate of
my family. Can you
imagine what it was
like to be one of them,
to be built like them,
to talk like them
to have the benefits
of being born into such
a wealthy and powerful
American family. I went
to the best schools,
had all kinds of tutors
and trainers, travelled
widely, met the famous,
the controversial, and
the not-so-admirable
and I knew from
a very early age that
if there were ever any
possibility of escaping
the collective fate of this famous
Boston family I would
take that route and
I have. I hopped

on an Amtrak to New
York in the early
'70s and I guess
you could say
my hidden years
began. I thought
Well I'll be a poet.
What could be more
foolish and obscure.
I became a lesbian.
Every woman in my
family looks like
a dyke but it's really
stepping off the flag
when you become one.
While holding this ignominious
pose I have seen and
I have learned and
I am beginning to think
there is no escaping
history. A woman I
am currently having
an affair with said
you know you look
like a Kennedy. I felt
the blood rising in my
cheeks. People have
always laughed at
my Boston accent
confusing "large" for
"lodge," "party"
for "potty." But
when this unsuspecting
woman invoked for

the first time my
family name
I knew the jig
was up. Yes, I am,
I am a Kennedy.
My attempts to remain
obscure have not served
me well. Starting as
a humble poet I
quickly climbed to the
top of my profession
assuming a position of
leadership and honor.
It is right that a
woman should call
me out now. Yes,
I am a Kennedy.
And I await
your orders.
You are the New Americans.
The homeless are wandering
the streets of our nation's
greatest city. Homeless
men with AIDS are among
them. Is that right?
That there are no homes
for the homeless, that
there is no free medical
help for these men. And *women*.
That they get the message
—as they are dying—
that this is not their home?
And how are your
teeth today? Can

you afford to fix them?
How high is your rent?
If art is the highest
and most honest form
of communication of
our times and the young
artist is no longer able
to move here and speak
to her time . . . Yes, I could,
but that was 15 years ago
and remember—as I must
I am a Kennedy.
Shouldn't we all be Kennedys?
This nation's greatest city
is home of the business-
man and home of the
rich artist. People with
beautiful teeth who are not
on the streets. What shall
we do about this dilemma?
Listen, I have been educated.
I have learned about Western
Civilization. Do you know
what the message of Western
Civilization is? I am alone.
Am I alone tonight?
I don't think so. Am I
the only one with bleeding gums
tonight. Am I the only
homosexual in this room
tonight. Am I the only
one whose friends have
died, are dying now.
And my art can't

be supported until it is
gigantic, bigger than
everyone else's, confirming
the audience's feeling that they are
alone. That they alone
are good, deserved
to buy the tickets
to see this Art.
Are working,
are healthy, should
survive, and are
normal. Are you
normal tonight? Everyone
here, are we all normal.
It is not normal for
me to be a Kennedy.
But I am no longer
ashamed, no longer
alone. I am not
alone tonight because
we are all Kennedys.
And I am your President.

Maxfield Parrish
1995

MAXFIELD PARRISH

Often I turn on people
in rather strange &
inexplicable ways.
The source of
the irritation
escapes me.
It always has.
Sometimes
my heart just
opens and
gets called
back to some
other corner
of the cave.
You'd probably
laugh at the
flowers I
bought tonight.
Bluish purple
& they don't
even have
a name. "Name?"
pronounced the
man at the
fruit stand
he shook
his head
& laughed.

These purple
flowers have
no name. &
no smell. But
the room

smelled & looked
different when
I brought them
in with me.
For instance
I was gentle
with their
stems while
I thought
about how
many lovers
have told
me I'm
rough. These
are hearty
thick stems
yet I slipped
the elastic
off their
limbs as
if I were
a servant
undressing
the president's
child. Just
thinking of her
for once. Oddly
alive & being
touched by
me in this
practical way.
The whole thing's
off-kilter the
way my purple

flowers grow.
Something that
makes sense
in February.
I have enough sense
to buy flowers
now. But such
strange ones.
Sprayed. Their
eerie color
is not real.
At least not all of it.
Maybe none of
it. The eerie
little branches
from which
piney green leaves
grow & I guess
that's real. But
the 287,
no I mean
thousands
of faintly blue bells
I can hardly see
I must be getting old
up close they make me feel dizzy
the fineness, the wealth of this pseudo-life
tiny balls, pale blue
with a sliver of a tongue
sticking out or sometimes
everything's teeny & sexual
it's sort of like underpants
a cover or a case
that's purple & the little

ball is blue.
I don't know why this wave
of a plant belongs in my vase.
I needed something fake to
start me up. Something
I could be gentle
with just to try.
Looking hard I say Baby
I don't know why I can
give you everything
& I'm dazzled by your frown.

BLEEDING HEARTS

Know what
I'm jealous of?
Last night.
It held
us both
in its
big black
arms
& today
I hold
between
my legs
a shivering
pussy.
Bleeding &
shaking
wet with
memory
grief & relief.
I don't know
why the universe
chose me
to be female
so much beauty
& pain,
so much
going on
inside
all this
change
everywhere
coins falling
all over
the bed

& death
is a dream.
Deep in
the night
with thousands
of lovers
the sucking
snapping
reeling
flesh
deep in
the cavity
of endless
night across
mounds
of bodies
I peer over
is it
love or
war. The hollow
creeping
cheek
where
I was
born.

SLEEPLESS

I came in tonight and my building sighed.
It was a beautiful woman stretching in
the morning. All blue and blonde and
gauzy white. My dreams of you are always
softer than you are. My dreams
must need a goddess and it seems she has
your face. And so you may stay a while
in my heart. My image of your languorous
arms and fists slowly stretching through
the early day as if Monday were another
sleepless woman's body. Two of you
to make the universe complete.
The embrace of you makes my day
so sweet because I am the author
of this sport. The other woman is dark
and green and curly, full of rocks
and sauce and dark lights hanging

in the sky. She's the sound of a
yawning cave. She pulls me down
and makes me whisper evil and
violent wishes, makes me spank
her with a whip and fierce
rules and fond names to cage
her in. How could everything
shrink so—these women dancing
in my mind. What holds the world together
for anyone else—blind women, white
men, frightened Chinese boys. I guess I
have a hunger that's stronger than
toast, I wouldn't say most
because the shapeless woman hanging
over my shoulder says I mustn't.
She shows me with her eyes which are water.
She tells me with her breath, incredible,
a hurricane, a disaster.
Her teeth are sparkling
ruin, her tongue a poison

snake, her throat
an endless fall
onto a meadow of warm sushi.
And lakes of blood and
green birds swooping
and singing.

And dawn, a dawn
that's unrecognizable.
It's there I finally
stopped in your
midnight arms.

What could lead
me this way,
what furry
balconies await me. What amber
yawns what plentiful breasts
diving between the legs
of God to see a mirror
an amazing pond, a one-eyed
man inside you cleaning
the kitchen with a sparkling
knife. I step on his face
and snap his back in two
with my finger and you
reward me with
heartthrob and
I never do come back.
I want you home with
me. I want you alone
with me. I wish you
would get lost
so I could walk the world
with my women.
I would call your name
everywhere. Wouldn't
that be enough, even

better. There is a woman
in the flower. Millions
of women hiding in the trees.
You will never miss me.
There is a universe
of color for you to
feed from. Before
I leave you I will
open its legs
with my sword.

I always put my pussy
in the middle of trees
like a waterfall
like a doorway to God
like a flock of birds
I always put my lover's cunt
on the crest
of a wave
like a flag
that I can
pledge my
allegiance
to. This is my
country. Here,
when we're alone
in public.
My lover's pussy
is a badge
is a night stick
is a helmet
is a deer's face
is a handful
of flowers
is a waterfall
is a river
of blood
is a bible
is a hurricane
is a soothsayer.
My lover's pussy
is a battle cry
is a prayer
is lunch
is wealthy

is happy
is on teevee
has a sense of humor
has a career
has a cup of coffee
goes to work
meditates
is always alone
knows my face
knows my tongue
knows my hands
is an alarmist
has lousy manners
knows her mind

I always put
my pussy in the middle
of trees
like a waterfall
a piece of jewelry
that I wear
on my chest
like a badge
in America
so my lover & I
can be safe.

SHHH

I don't think
I can afford the time to not sit right down &
write a poem about the heavy lidded
white rose I hold in my hand
I think of snow
a winter night in Boston, drunken waitress
stumble on a bus that careens through
Somerville the end of the line
where I was born, an old man
shaking me. He could've been my dad.
You need a ride? Wait, he said.
This flower is so heavy in my hand.
He drove me home in his old blue
Dodge, a thermos next to me,
cigarette packs on the dash
so quiet like Boston is quiet
Boston in the snow. It's New York
plates are clattering on St. Mark's
Place. Should I call you?
Can I go home now
& work with this undelivered
message in my fingertips
It's summer
I love you.
I'm surrounded by snow.

THE MIRROR IS MY MOTHER

If I'm not in there I'm in here
the city accordion in someone's kind
hands, squeeze in, pull out,
holds us closely on the couch.
The mirror is moved
and I'm facing the wall, let me turn
quickly and turn to the city. The beauty
of Christmas is accidental,

      a legion of scarves getting
off, and cars, paintings, movements,
a Cardinal aghast, turning the pages
of the *New York Times* they had lived
together for quite a few years
both happened to be standing there
when the Berlin Wall fell down.

As I watched her lying there,
shriveled, the huge head decorated
and the room swayed with candles
and white flowers and as I said
it was as if you moved a mirror
and what you saw was the wall
instead. My uncle's lips looked
rubber, smeared all over
his poor old Irish face.
It was his voice I knew, not his
lips. Poor old Uncle Tim who
always wiggled his ears. Aunt Ann always
so huge in power and strength,
strangled by grief, a little
pooch, dependent on her grandchildren
who loved her. I say death is a strange
thing. I want to stay open to this

life, my rubber lips twisting
in lies and fear, my eyes burning
with impatience and truth.
An angel should come and they would
speak. On my birthday they were handing me
millions of pictures of myself, as they
do in our culture, the clapping of
hands, lights, everything that's not
dead and dark. I brought my ancient
bunny home from Boston, the puppets
I brought my mask. Now this African woman
looks down on my life, poor and white
outside the christian lights blink
comically onto my tenement bed.
In East Friesia the lightning means
they're taking your picture again.
Don't squint, let your mother
look at your beautiful face and love
you for breath and movement and
hearing an animal suddenly moving
in the brush let it pass.
Never strike.

EN GARDE

All the hills & the trees
and the woman
chopping wood
outside &
the lazy
dog. I am
dedicated
to this. Its existence.
The marinade.
The veterans
of wars up the
hill popping
off their
gun, dreaming
of Iraq.
They can go
there if they'd
like to
go. In a state of War
a man can understand
what a woman
means by
space.
All the
homosexuals
are word-
processing.
Not going
to war.
All you
have
to say
is I'm Gay
& you can

stay in
America
forever. Just
think about
how it's
felt for
me to
be female
in America.
Or in
this world.
Any man
would
kill a
man,
certainly
be exonerated
in court
for killing
a man
who was
gay &
came on
to him
that way,
you know
sexual.

Every day
I get
treated
that way.
Mmm I like those tits.
Has George Bush

ever been
flattered
walking down
the streets
for his
big balls
so scrumptious.

I look up
and I
face a square
of clouds
packed
in blue.
My friend
is so lucky
to own
this barn.
Am I in
America
while
I'm writing
this
poem?

My tongue &
lips are
in America.
So's my
dog who
I love.
My car.
That wreck,
my ultimate

female karma
spilling over
into the
male space
like acid
if they
had to
be me
for a
moment
the beauty &
the beast
they could
read my
face, they
would know
their place
they would
give me
space,
they would
lower their
guns &
beg for
water.

PV

Some old drunk who'd been
to France recently died, left
his collection of Isherwood, John
O'Hara, tobacco-stained, grungy
with tattered invites hanging out.
I come wagging out of the train
station at 59th & nearly scream,
Just the books I need!

I take my own sense of
abundance down
into the subway, the
F, Second Ave., the
bodies strewn, the
stink of human
shit the ungodly
lights, standing, waiting
in the heat

The mother won't repeat
for the child. If you
didn't get it the first
time . . .

Who is that Irish novelist
he says, the one we see
in meetings in East Hampton

the train arrives & I hop

on that lesbian poet, the
one we always see around
3:30 in Kiev, having a very
late lunch I guess.

We whiz uptown to get help.
We whiz back down. This
is an old fashioned phone
call, Do you have
10 bucks, All saints' day 1989.

I slept with her last night,
first time since August, she's
moving so the smells of her
neighbor's pot won't waft
insidiously into her bedroom
anymore, Jan with his
new electric piano, Jan the
monkey-faced pot dealer who
teaches tai chi.

I went to see 17 art shows on
Saturday. 17. That's not a lot.
Saw Tim in the hospital on Sun-
day. Thin Tim. We know he'll
come out. He doesn't want to
be everyone's friend Tim who has AIDS
so we won't let him be that.
We won't.
We charged around in our
dungarees watching the century
approach. Another one, nicer
than this, young again, full
of conviction, naïveté, covered

with hair and sunlight, brim-
ming with time, a wave of
invention . . .

I take my sense of abundance
into the subway & what do
I see? People bending reading
swaying, torn posters
waving in a song of
sickening movement. Why don't
they think we know about
rice, racing . . . handsome woman
fiddling with her bag. We're
the same people who met in
a disaster, but nothing hap-
pened here. You can't call
it joy this somnolence, licking
our lips with our earphones
on. The poet got off
in the yellowing light,
the rising tile, then
Lexington Ave. Have you
gone here, did you
go there everyone wants
to know. & there's the
EXIT. Absolutely now
I'm going & the buildings
are growing before my
eyes.

LOOKING OUT, A SAILOR

The clouds looked made, & perhaps
they were. An angry little shelf
for the moon to have
some influence
on. I'm dying tomorrow

my car died tonight
a glorious explosion
then clunk.

Turning pages, turning pages
coming up on midnight
when the poet died.

It was his heart
not his
head.

The girl, she was say 27
covered in tattoo
a sauce her
boyfriend
made to cover
her sins

let's say she is glad tonight
to be dead. Her name?
Lorri Jackson.

So I push on & my
dog needs
a bath—don't sell Rosie
short says the

trainer & flattered
I won't

I remember the last
night with my
car. Came home
& called the night
watery grave. Didn't
know why. Everyone
dying around
me now. But
not yet,
not me yet.

The lights all smeared &
gooey in an incredible
downpour like Lorri's
body I could see shadows
that I think were
persons, they were
the dead &
we were
alive, yes I think
it was that
way that
last night. So lucky
I didn't hit
one.

My pooch
by my side. This
is my life
when I grow

up I thought
as a child.
In my boat with
my dog, named
what, Rosie,
she barks
driving into
the night

god, we
couldn't
see a thing
but we weren't
scared. Besides
we'd had
plenty of
life.

Prayed for a
parking space.
Funny turning
in the dark
those lights
back there
are cars I think.
Don't ask me
said Rosie.

But I wanted to sail
the rest of my
life. It was dumb.
I'd arrived
there was

my space.
Perfect & I pulled in
& this is the
saddest poem
I ever wrote.
What can I tell you about
sadness, the shapes
you find beneath it,
how you run from
it in your sleep,
bolting awake

early in my labors I
worked with
children, I was one
then but so
what the story goes.
Autistic kids, a
boy named
Bobby
who so loved
porcelain he leaned
his cheek on
it, a little
animal & his
cool white
mama

the things I warm my
hands by are not
true, someone
who holds her
head like

that forbidding
I think
is warm

I would lay my paw
on her icy bottle,
her icy dead
cheek, her red
legs

the red light rippled
in my watery grave
if I could paint
tonight I would
be the word
that fills the silence
after modern
following something
slow, red
changing lanes
it was utterly
silent my
painting, the
dog breathing
well, relentlessly
& they had
pulled my antennae
off long ago so
deep down
there was
some music
classical,
how to say
I was having

the pivotal
moment of
my life
with a
dog, all
the silence
had led up to
here & streamers
could be
followed to
the moment
of my
death,

what kind
could I be
some kind of
poet who
followed it
along, say it's
distant & far
off, or
right next
to me
now, I
do not know
or choose
to. I saw
the world
melt all
at once

I want to
go with

everyone
waiting for
everything
to shift back
to real &
it's stranger
& stranger
now—all
of my lies don't
lie anymore.
The car dies
& I drive
on. The rain
stops. He said
I would
surely outlive
my dog &
I know
that & I
took her
home. But
everyone. No I
didn't know
that. When
everyone
goes I
go. I'm
following
now, &
our truth
is dark

A DEBATE WITH A GLOVE

John Higgins, Mary McCluskey
what about them? I flashed
my palm and wagged it.
The personality as the
site of spiritual advancement
what about my book?
Spirituality & Sexuality,
that's all. Make the young dogs
pay. A play is an opportunity
to do something visual.
My vision. Here let me straighten
these shirts. Eileen spoke
so well about the creative
process. Maybe she would
like to do it again.

What about those monuments?
The beggar & the priest.
The weight of my cunt.
Let me walk the streets of Baghdad.
Are these breasts mine?
What kind of problem is a poem.
We don't get to choose what
kind of spiritual experience we
have. We don't get to choose
our orgasm. We don't
even get to choose our
lover. What happened to me.
Who was she.
Are they bedbugs.
Take me to Delhi fast.
I itch.
At five my soul wants to be
alone. With the world &

its armies. With my
sex. With my hands
with my beautiful
hands. She had
been turned
into a deity
in the end.
First she vanished,
then she was
that.
I know what kind
of god
I'd like to be.
A blue god.
A blue god man.
Those men, they make
me want to dance.
Tell me something else.
Was I married.
Have I been here
before. Why am I
always in between.
Is it late or
is it early.
Money, I could
give a shit.
Fame, forget it.
An authenticity
that rattles
my bones. Is
it two of
everything
or one.
Is it none.

I'm sorry we
went to war
with you &
broke your
bridge.
I'll fix it now.
Really. Should
we get married
or something?
I'm very
smart. Oh
you don't
think so.
Well. Maybe
I'll write
a poem. Suddenly
I don't care
that I'm
gonna
die. Even
the bed keeps
me awake.
The breeze
of the world.
It opened
my jar.
It called
me home.
It said,
Lucifer!

LATE MARCH

Tons of purple
out today.
Think I'll
take a
walk &
collect
some. An
old damp
shirt, dull
dog leash
nearly magenta.
The shrieks
of the
boys
when they
play
ball. Really
vaguely
lilac.
Your eyes.
Nope. While
you lay
in bed.
The purple
of separation.
Time, mauve.
Days go
by. The
boink
of the
ball as
the moments
pass in
the lazy

orchid
of Sunday
when nothing's
right,
nothing's
wrong &
I snap
on your
dark
purple
collar &
take you
home. No
reason
to cry.

YOU

Perhaps I can sell my point of
view I thought looking up at
the trees. The white rot on
the elm reminds me of tears

          A stream
of tiny tiny green dots
covers the sidewalk,
a grey parquet
floor of octagons. Now that
I'm gone I only want to
climb up on you
cause you're it, put my
fingers on your dark brown
hills, the buses that flood
your small streets, beeping
I turned the faucet
now everything is loss

She is like some kind of daughter to the
world, prince of its gates & fences
little squirrel nuzzling up to its roots

It's inconsequential which way I go
the breeze hits me like other
clouds of dust & "why bother"
to this sadness that
surrounds a small green
heart connected by soft fuzzy
roots to its borders that used
to stick to something but
they fell this spring, two-dimensionally
alone in the wind, and
it's silly to name the wind

too. A while ago we used
to have some gods & they
had stories that explained
the way they were. We
talk about stories
now the way they stop &
start say no no no
you can't hurt me now
I'm not here anymore.

"NO POEMS"

It was
a little
golden
cross,
wooden
like a ruler,
really. Wrapped
round
with pink
flowers.
Then Ann,
she put
a small
cut glass
vase of
more pink
flowers,
she leaned
across
the hole
she couldn't
quite, it
was awk-
ward
so the
monk
took the
vase and
placed
it for
her at
the foot
of the
cross,

& things
were even
moreso.
There
was a
hole in
the ground
& in it
the can.
We were
invited
to take
a hand-
ful of
dirt, earth
the name
of
our planet,
& throw it
on our
friend whose
burnt
remains
were in
the can. It
felt good,
cold, strong,
old, a
handful
of planet.
Here, I
thought &
wiped my
hand on

the brown
bandana
Duncan
brought. I
wiped the
dirt from
my hand.
My friend
was buried
under a
tree. Little
cross, stroke
of sun
hitting its
shiny gold.
We stood
in a circle,
the friends,
the monks,
brown.
One monk
lifted a
spade &
shoveled
it in, earth
to fill
the hole
& now he
was gone.
We stood.
It was
pretty
as a
picture & he

was
taking
photographs
the whine
of the
camera &
then we
stood
still. We'll
probably
come
back said
Duncan. *Huh!*
That's
what I
was just
thinking.

LIFE

My sense of preservation
a gift borne to me by
my mother through
the days of
her world has
led me to
wrap bread
in plastic. Occasionally
fruit, a lime,
may sit split
in the spattered
refrigerator
door, there to
dry and get
like plastic.
But never
bread. Bread
must live.
I wish I had
a collection of
plastic things
to put all
other things
in—little bits
of food
that I
would keep
longer. Eat
later. But
not living
food like
tomatoes. No,

I mean
bread. Why
do I fear
the demise
of bread
so much
its drying
up & hardening.
Surely I
think it's
some kind
of body.
Bread's so
cheap & so
is flesh, really.
There's so much
of it daily
marching through
the streets of
my world. But
is it my world
really. I'm
just another
loaf of
bread in
shoes, marking
time. I sat
on a stoop
this afternoon
in front
of a camera
trying to

make a
glowing
impression
that would
last &
travel far.
An important
crumb. When
I read
books I
think of
my cunt. If it's
about love
of God, the
hotter I
get. I better
clean some
things up
I think
putting the
corpses of
the things
I eat
onto little
shelves. I
shut the
door &
the light
goes out.
I am God.

THE POET

I made myself into a poet because it was the first thing I really loved. It was an act of will. I realize that now. I was always afraid of asking for things from the devil. I would probably get them. Then I stumbled onto this idea about the purity of the heart. This is a way I could get what I want. To desire one thing, that's the idea. I knew I could do that. And I already knew what I wanted. To keep doing what I was doing, but to know that it was true. It was right for me to keep doing that, to want nothing else but that. I felt free at last. My life had become a dream. My dream. My life was the cloth of that. Days spent sharing an egg with a cat were good days. With my little red floor & white walls. & millions of men in my bed. It meant nothing. I liked alcohol. What poet didn't. I woke up in the dreaming poem of the day & made myself a hot black cup of coffee. I would begin. Soon I would want something. A cigarette. That was good. The place I bought them was far enough, a walk, good for my body, something blue for my hand. Who did I think the poet was. A talking dog. Who felt her lips with her fingertips & wrote that down. You see the page for me has terrific dimension. I can go into the white & I do. The lines are designs for something real, how much space around the slender bars I bend and shape in the name of my world. A comma is a little fish, a dash sort of a raft. When we say capitals do we mean apples. German words about the same size as God. When you want to refer to that. Its comedy. Sometimes the poem wants to come home. It has a firm back, its left hand margin, sometimes it feels just fine about that. The page is the sky. My typewriter, classic, a wispy one had no spine & so my poems floated like clouds, globs of sunlessness & I marked the world free. Sensationally flat poems I know each line went from there to there was ironic as print felt that way soothed by the cruelty of wasps and was crisper than them, just a season of flat poems. Lonely the loss of rock 'n roll. It was receding. My poems were flat. A woman made me ache, I was love on the page not yet I had always felt like a brick shit house. I was the poem. The incident in the afternoon the folded sheet, I was the mouth the sounds emitted from I was the pipes of god, me this structure in eternity. Enter it. The oldest dream I remember an important one was about a train in the night going to Germany & I must get on & save myself. Once in a while I say be full, and it is, be slow, oh tear holes in me as the day dies. I have truly become my poems, but do note the sculpture of others, their obliviousness, like architects leaving crumbs. It is not lost our century, thanks to us. We are the liars & thieves, we are the women we are the women I am full of holes because you are. I am the only saintly man in town. Don't be afraid to be feminine. A girl on a rowboat, full of holes. She saw words shooting through.

School of Fish
1997

SCHOOL OF FISH

Everything's equal now. Blue leash blue bike
blue socks covering my ankles today
what about my friend: "I never wear socks"
for a week or two she lived in the streets &
it was such an illumination. What's this human
addiction to light. One morning I dreamt about
homelessness, joked about it. Life reduced
or expanded to getting doggie her very
next can. Dog's inexcusable addiction to
eating. At the bottom of the sea, David said,
the fishies are inexcusably addicted to light.
Same day I and my dog were left on the street.
No home, no keys, streams of pouring grey
rain. Now what is this grey, in relationship
to blue. Ask some painter is it less light
or is it what. What kind of hat should
I have worn yesterday in my crisis.
The dog's blue leash was gone. My feet reaching
over the bounds of the sidewalks, its curbs
and waves, pavement splashing up
hard and grey. Where did I see that man?
Someplace so human they even had one of *them*.
In a dark blue teeshirt, laughing. There is nothing
to my anecdote, my predicament, my color
crisis. There is nothing but blue & grey.
A glint hits the golden key, and it's a bad one
not the original and I kept turning and turning
there were copies everywhere in the neighborhood
that's what I am trying to say. I simply walked
and the apologies kept coming streaming in
and I said I simply walked and the tree
turned, no the key and the bottom of the sea
is flooded with light, we just get used to it
the deeper and deeper we go and the harder

it is to turn the key and eventually we
go and it is very very dark
we just get used to the light
but the blues and the greys and the feelings
of lostness, it's like home, it's like family.

ROAD WARRIOR

What happens when you
contain the flame?

I stuck my head out
the window & waved
at the stars.

Wait for me, I'm coming
I'm coming home.

LAST SUPPER

It was Wednesday night &
the food was so hot
the tree sat undecorated
I watched the men
in the take out
shop, felafel men
spoon sauce generously
and I thought make
it good for me
it is my last supper.
The shape of the
little tomatoes
what is that
shape, oval
like an eye
the bottom
of the boat
a death boat
Connie pointed it out
embedded in
the architecture
of the Guggenheim
uptown, death
tucked in all
its wise corners.
I missed out
on Peggy's house
in Venice
one day
the day it was
closed. Look
through the black
gate of Peggy's
house. Hi Peggy

Dead at 138.
Can I tell you
what I ate
today? Besides
the felafel
platter I had
a bird's nest
& then, uh,
a slice and
before that
let's see am I boring
you to death?
I had a couple
of bananas, little
too ripe, bright
yellow, some
cheese & crackers
beige & blue
I had
oh I had
some banana
bread, tan.
And you know
what I thought
at the
gym tonight
I really thought
it. It was
really bright &
I was naked
I was standing
in the shower
like a mooing
cow, staring

into the
light & I
thought, life,
Peggy, life
is the only
privilege. And
the only
real toast
is food.

MERK

There's too much light in my life
there that's better
the street people recommend
don't let your brother fling his
leg & arm around you like
you're his girlfriend. Humpin your
kneecap, stuff like that
the vilest smell of all tonight
is human food
it's November when the moons switch
places. White is bad
black is good. Food stinks.
Carrying their buckets of soup
to their stupid abodes
furs around their necks, beasts.
What do humans eat? Dogs, more or less.
Ripping fruit from the vine
snipping the crop
maybe vegetables would like to
let their baby be too
and never never eat the human
that is a crime. Push my machine
to see what nazi called
me. Go out and kill her with my teeth

I'm a bored outsider
the season is cold
everywhere doors are slamming
and look who you're in the
room with now. Someone to eat
I hope. Think of Goethe
Werner Goethe with his leg
flung up on a rock in
Italy. Take a bite

of that fat calf.
He's like a big posing gondola
what's the idea
every poet I know is a partial artist
the lucky ones are dead
naturally incomplete
but look at everyone you think of
hanging on to some misapprehended
particle of modernism, all
plumped up with pillows
there's nothing
after a modern idea
for poets. All they do
is think & eat. If you call
that making something
& I don't, I don't call that art.
We must offer ourselves
up as food or eat
someone. If you can make there
be less of someone else
or someone could take
a bite out of you
then you can join in the incompletion
or excess of your age
I'm sick of seeing dunces celebrated
that's the job
someone that looks
good in ribbons
someone surrounded
by their editor's
arms. Love object
of a lesbian
but not being
one. Particle board

potential screen
play, plastic
hair, translates
well, millions will hold
you on the train
bite me now
bite me forever
in your two strong

o eat me read
me something

I am the daughter
of substitution
my father fell
instead of the dresser
it was the family
joke, his death
not a suicide
but a joke

how could I accidentally
get eaten
slipping into your
sandwich or refrigerator
sort of a dick
that crawls
up from the bottom of your
ice cream cone

it's too late for some
of us, but for others
it's never late
enough. Tonight

when they moved
the lights and everything
looked completely
horrible for
a change
I was looking
for sympathy
and you asked
me for the menu

I have escaped the unseemly
death of the alcoholic
yet I keep my ear so close
to the ground & I know
what they know
I begin to smell
funny, another fate

it was if I was falling
last night
but I imagined
myself a bit
of food
& I was safe
in your mouth
& I would
never die

it is the legacy
of my family
to change in the air
& smash as
something
new

not a woman
but a chair
full of flowers

not a poet
but a donut
or a myth

go up there
& get me a cracker
darling
& proudly
I walked

PORN POEMS

Her tongue & her
heart were
throbbing
in the holster
of her pussy.

JUST GOD

We know the city
hates us as we
sit in our
vanilla
stained rooms.
Flick Flick. The
media ruins
our lives so we
build tunnels
in our poems
to help the
darkness in,
to give truth
to ruin, crud
to our poems.
Resist the world
resist the poem
surrender to me
today. I know something
I know love
informed by heaven
daily it's blue.
The constancy
is the thing I
love in the brownness
watch the day
harden request
to a sparrow.

Day
or jail?
Think of it perfect.
How feelable. If
this isn't heaven

what is? Inching
time. Darkness
of jacket goes
on, those
wavering
fronds. Repeating
the names of
my enemies.
Why? Is he
a prayer.
Door close.
                    She
saw the shapes
a simple shape.
It isn't
art. It helps.
Is it
clean? I'm learning
again. The day
is a window.
The day is watchful.
All we need.

MR. TWENTY

Everywhere I look
there's another bottle
of sparkling water
it's the new beer
new since 1978 or so.
Not so new.
Even the millennium is unspeakably silent
having been here so long
100 years of the naked emperor
is more than my eyes
can stand. His little penis
bobbing below his
big belly, his tiny toes
in small loafers.
Won't somebody stop
this man. The first thing we learned
was the world would end
in our time. Do you think
we give a shit by now
Lying at the bottom of the
toilet of the naked
emperor, every time
he flushes we're supposed
to applaud. We do not.
We yawn. That was a
really big turd the emperor
just made. Must be
for women we giggled.
Huh. I lifted my
glass to my lips
it's mostly silence now
the regular darkening
as he puts his fanny
down on the lid of the
century. It makes me just

want to do something great
for the world. If there's
another big race riot in
America I think I'll go
direct streetcar named
desire in the midst of
it. I'm sick of doing nothing
I want to help.
Naturally I'll play Stanley
an angry white lesbian
walking through the burning
streets yelling Stella
Yeah. I'm eager. I'm rubbing
my palms. No seriously
folks I was born
just a few years after the
Emperor put some big bombs
down. It was very
fertile ground. I remember
a screaming sound in the
sky but the world seemed silent
that day & then some
ashes fell, or maybe it
was a scrap of worn out
rubber from the side
of the road
somehow it fell from
the sky. It filled
with papers books
& clothes. Well how *do* I
feel about the end of
the world. He's become
beautiful to us. Look
at his color. Kind of
tawny pink. Little bits

of hair on his chest
streams of it pouring
down his legs & a
slight smile on his
thin lips. It's graceful the
way he just walks
around gazing at us
and you know why he has no
clothes. It's the ultimate
power stroke—to
show the world how you
start your morning
before they see
you, I am this
simply breast
and shoulders
forearms, slightly bulgy
waist thighs amply on
the chair, legs
crossed. Step out
& say I have no job
no interest really
in engaging, but must walk
and spin, an unclothed
lily, & you will greet
me with silence
my beforeness
my adamant
unbeginning to trample
all of you with my big ass
daily, to take that royal
ride on my own
for days and weeks till
the lie is the utter complicitude
of every living thing that

has seen me, the man,
the naked emperor
smiling at you fools. I'm
the beaming man on the motorcade
the man in the suit with
promises, my Dad,
to look into his eyes
and see myself
smiling.

The only wild thing
well we tried that for a while
some kind of truth
the only wild thing
is to complain & complain
about his nakedness
his ugly fucking naked body
marching up & down the world
making everyone pretend
to believe in him
it's more than I can
stand. I would
evacuate. But
he's everywhere.
Shitting on our heads &
our couches
children can't even see him
I mean that's a problem
Am I wrong?
It would be: in my time
there was nothing else
we gave up the fight
he was everywhere
the Sun

AURORA

I come from a long line of worshippers of strong crazy women
I have been holding you
walking along the clouds that hover over the Neva
and as each screaming teakettle arrives
at a point that's clean of disease,
the moment boiled away
and as the red velvet curtain whisked
to either side
down seams of cruelty you cried
I kept sweeping you clean of meaning
and light

in Mockba
as each pedestal of the worker glistens as the trains
vanish every fifty seconds
LED agree
and spinning chandeliers of imperiality meet waning
soviation and incremental candy bar express
is on its way and the middle
range is absent. It's either the very old and singular
way too pricey, shiny stuff, or a commonplace that can't be
lifted easily and in between it's
gone that's why we're here. Pushing palms
against the columns, fists empty of blue cans of gin
averring snickers and vouching for pelmany
huge moon water, voda, Da Da.

At the font of your resolution to stuff a rug in a bag
make too late dinners for no one
in the weakness & the wentness
I have been holding you
in the gentle tomboy's tears
zipping sounds, success! Only a river could take you home

zharka boots, having utterly no interest in Dostoevsky's
being open to instant messages
being a brick in the family pattern
long ranging flight pattern
understanding vertigo but not now

realizing to take the picture
I know what gerunds are
crying through dinner very satisfying
know what else?
I know the cups you wanted were
a loving cup of lying there forever
on that train.

WOO

out in a bus stop
among the
mountains
a yawn, boy drive by
blue mountains
little tan mountain
house, similar
each scape
is all its own place
no woman
is like any
other

ROTTING SYMBOLS

Soon I shall take more
I will get more light
and I'll know what I think
about that

Driving down Second Ave. in a car
the frieze of my hand
like a grandmother
captured in an institution
I know I'll never live here again etc.
many many long years ago
Millions of peeps in the scrawl
the regular trees
the regular dog snort &
dig. In the West Village
you could put on a hat
a silly hat & it's clear
whereas over here
20 years passed
that rotting hat
it's loyalty to someone or something
that's really so gone
the moment clenched
like religion or government.

Wait a minute. I prefer
umm a beatle's cap
when it's really really old
neighborhood devoted to that.

Poetry is a sentimental act
everything spring she said
being surrounded by so much rot.
Pages & pages

mounds of them that I'm in
not some library but in your
little home, like you.
Every season I know I'm leaving
I'm as loyal as the cross
to this smeltering eccentricity
down by the river with Daddio
toss your ball in the river
in the future over bridges
they say you have to imagine
the 20th century. All these buildings were colored
a blasted interior
scarlet curtains rattling day
cobwebs on inexplicable machinery
a theater once dwelled here
all I see is rotting ideas
the epics I imagined
the unified cast of everyone
eating turkey together
on a stage
my idea
like water towers popping up
feeling mellow
not exactly nothing all this time
but the buildings that are absolute
gone that I never
described. You can't kill
a poet. We just get erased &
written on. It aches in
my brain, my back
this beauty I'm eating my toast
everyone I knew you would
be dead tomorrow
& you were. The composing camera

infatuated with the shovel
on the lid & the pile
of rocks. He is not aging
same Alexandrian
blond in Binibon's
the sirens are gods
when I lifted my head
from my swarming difficulty
You were so marvelous
bringing those toys to my feet
in between the invisibility of
the constant production & consumption
the network of that
& apart from the mold.
You survived.

SULLIVAN'S BRAIN

If there's a person in the paintings
say a boy and a dog on the beach
they call it narrative
no cute jokes
the head is talking now
you can name a cloud in Latin
you can name a wind
in Shakespeare
when "it" soliloquizes
do we turn & whisper
bill speaks
I like the crunch of
Rosie's jaw on
science diet
the caw of her
throat but
my language tends
to personalize
in the Rain
dog's name
the name of the product
it contains
the ker-clump
"I must go out"

Peepers attend
the newly configured yard
where a tree fell
down & lies there
& a virgin who observed
my coming out
just stares & creeps
say whatever's peeping
out. Its beauty is

beyond me. I start
backing my car up
you girls & your structuralism
post haste have taught
me so much. The angry
dog shaking shaking
the metonymic
bird. Not daughter
but slaughter.
I left the ghetto
I'm standing way out
the black & the prongs of light
surrounding me
doodling in Nature
There is no one
on my beach
normality is a dot
morphing away
every single cunt
began to feel like a movie
the cameras are rolling,
Love. To stay here
or there.
I like,
No I can't
say that.

In the sickest
morning I ever
saw a structure, a totem
growing in your tiny
house, a green
thing, the smile

of arousal
like an em-dash of a beach
it's too easy for you
to be pretty I tell them
we all know birds
squeak & cry

Wiggly
describes my
desire, an
aesthetic
if we imagine a light source
somewhere & all the
leaves living &
the dead can be said
to be moving
before its big
loud eye
then we move
towards living in art
interfacing in awe
not orgasm
but is one
yeah but don't touch me again
I'm done. Finally the
dog settles down
I know rugs says bill
it's about threads I suppose
counting them
you need a good eye
I have a good gut
but my "I" is
wiggly as is my purse

her half hour
stretches so long
on a day like today
the radio at large
no beach
walking
up the steps
of my abstraction

MY WAR IS LOVE

I was moved
something that didn't happen in sex
happened in my eyes
I feel like some old veteran
you left your marks on me
I could feel the concessions
brewing storm clouds
in the distance
upstate New York & its stabbing
vistas
you can see the man who knew
so much had a lousy house
Thomas Cole
the other one had insurance
money
it makes a difference
you know Hartford, '91,
but nothing can protect us
from heartbreak
like weather
the death of a child
we walked through
their house
spotting views

As you move through
the house at
the sculpted trees
it was only death in their eyes
I think of the past that way
upstate New York
these men's big mansions
a little baby grave
I think of my love as a dead child

cunt like the barrel
of a gun
scraping myself against you
the words are gone
I'm watching my love grow
invisible
both my parents had
these tiny children
sisters & brothers
we never knew
every veronica makes me sad
a baby's grave is
like a little belly
baby graves in my eyes
if the most innocent
victims of a war

loved, most invisible
the pig won

and that makes me glad
the farmer had to dance
& the animals watched
but the pig had to sip
sip and survive
the pig in a house
I think about walking
in these houses
with you
that once upon a time
you would know that the sun
set there &
we had a river
the battle is lost I sob

in the middle of war
they twirled the house
round & round in
their heads
he died when the century
was one
each window was a perfectly
imagined day
when it rained the eyes cried
battered by weather
so many days
empty the trees &
the eyes see far
all the maroon fortunes
of the churches
the precious little family
like a life in a box
I was haunted by views
something that the rich
leave to be
sit down & smile around
the flapping of days
the windows close
and the day turns in
we light a lamp
in our eyes

WATERFALL

I miss whiskey
regular fun
meet a girl
know I'd won

I miss whiskey
what a dope
now I'm sober
horny,
broke

Whiskey I miss
you, I had
a friend
you're never alone
with an elbow
to bend

I play a guitar
but music stinks
I sit in nature
typical oinks

typical bahs, neighs
& whinny
typical doodle
bloooo
ka-thunk
ka-thunk

In me speaks
the divine
menagerie
the nectar
the blood on my hands

Girls Girls Girls!
I came to pray

TONIGHT

Just for the fuck of it
my arms are stripes
I fling them upwards
to be part of it, trees
to be one with all the things
in the world, sap,
rockets going up.

I'm pink & shiny round
a pale face
I'm a pearl, hear my
silence in the ponds
of the world, see my name
come dripping
out of my mouth like fish
drip out from my circle

Hey just for once
I felt the thing rising
in the rockets of my
fame, to pull in the limbs
my roots, quit the community
find my sandals
walk, save my self

millions of candles know our
distance, flower magic
hits of light dropping
down the trees of my game
everywhere is a kind of travel
every distance is me, you, when I go

in the woods a deer is moving
call me crunchy leaves
starry night, Mammy,
the ringing sounds of your hoofs
in the light in the woods
Tonight.

STORY

About a poet
you might
say—he's really
good at
being alone.
You might lie
low with your
head hanging
down
or look up at a shirt
on a door
that smells of her
& say she's gone
you might cry
either way
but one feels
better. I don't see
it that way, she said
on the phone
it's the truth
I said
I'm vanishing.

NO NO

Look I don't know
about getting
things back
a woman stands
in a room
& it's winter
she sees herself
there are 3 hot things
to tell her lover
soon the day
changes shape
not this bird
but it's different
the box stays
the room in her head
soon both heat
& winter are gone
I want to live
in my thoughts
of you, I believe
in you like a door
that returns

Skies
2001

Jonathan's
back from
the country
of Tod
and I'm
back too.

You get
out of work
on Irving
Place, I
mean everyone
at dusk
in this
long pause
and then
the green
eye

an old
game board
of lurches
and howls

I should
be so
secure
while
I'm riding
I am.

We deliver Coors
He's dead.

Matthew
Shepard's
simply
gone

little scarecrow
with his
scarecrow
desire

The whole mess
of it troubles me.
The sketchy little
lumps, they seem
inspired by the
area the moods
& clumps of trees
take, climbing up-
wards, it just goes
on its side, and
fills a lavish
area dead on,
it seems wolfish
the appetite of
this colony. It's
moving after all
and the boat
is plowing into
grey, heaping
piles of it on
the horizon, we
seem to be very
right, and
that's our immediate
future, hungry
grey not blue.

Doing the sky has
supplanted my
need for photographs.
It sit, the camera,
like a dark little
plug in my bag. The
sky meanwhile

is a sad blue green
just an inch of it.
Mostly full over that
a thin coarser ripple
of grey with thin
tears of a brighter
blue above. But we
still go right and
there is an arc in
the sky now, a
big blue one. It's
my hope & a
bird flies through it
and there's the
flag whapping in
its breeze,
the whirligigs in
the crow's nest
twirling & we see
houses and trees
the oily water,
red cranes, where's
my friend Lorraine
and a hint of
garnet is in

the cloud overhead.
There's clouds
painted on clouds
is rusty russet
the sky now, smooth
like old cream. There's
a small piece of
dark blue over

there to the right
but the boat
keeps turning away.
Our moments are
so damn fast the
turn of the boat
my clumsy pen
my heart beating

there's a sweet
white one like
a big fish, one
end just seems
to end—get
just a beat away,
a faint vertical
neighbor vaguer
or a funnel of
moving smoke
like industry or
the world

MY WIFE IS SHOPPING

You couldn't
mistake that
for happiness

his friends
helped
him down

and they began
hands on
the floor

same age

as my
father

one was
out in
the hall crying

sand, broken
glass
but it's
a kind
of happiness

four sad
gestures

she was
in both
accidents

it looked
like a shop
& I was

ashamed
disappointed

she said follow
me

and everything
collapsed
I hadn't
changed

I knew everyone

I was saved
from living

by these
boxes I
keep things
in

cities, ~~lives~~
~~histories~~

Twenty years ago
in May

no, don't do that
look at the crinkly
peach of the
sky in Chelsea
today

a man's foot
hits the
curb with
a phone at
his ear

it's dog walking
time

but mine
are away

I see a gleam
of cream
behind the
faintest netting
of trees

breeze, whistling
traffic

barely wet hair
from the
gym

that plane
overhead

& it's orange
again

WRITING

I can
connect

any two
things

that's
god

teeny piece
of bandaid

little folded
piece
of bandaid

I ran
to the
bathroom

to see
my face

sometimes
I don't
want to
see my
face in
the mirror

sometimes
I can't
bear
my thoughts

sometimes
I can't
do anything

but that's
okay

bandaid
book
god

that's
right

My mind's
pretty
juicy

pretty crayon-

y

Full moon.

THE CENTER

This is a place
where we can
just sit
flesh of a
caucasian colored
building

now don't
change your
mind

it's Allen St.

the sky is
my favorite
color
well one of
them

it's just something
in terms
of color
blue, certainly,

it's a very
wide cut
above dark
but this
blue has
such certainty
never more
blue than
this &
one

that is
soft

that's right
now lie
down
while I
see it through

the trees,
the tickling
hands of
my friends
my favorite
in the
world

I love
the ite
of favorite

when it
comes to
favoring
liking &
loving &
choosing all
your life
and
one sky
meets all
the trees
you've
ever known

in a long
squirt
of light &
it's still
not night

the lights
are neon
& we get
to rest

that's it
my animal
this broad
stoop is
a raft
I will
continue to
be young
until I'm
famous

and snug
in this
exactitude
the act
of waning
choosing

I'll write
while it's
light.

MILK

I flew into New York
and the season
changed
a giant burr
something hot was moving
through the City
that I knew
so well. On the
plane though it was
white and stormy
faceless
I saw the sun
& remembered the warning
in the kitchen
of all places
in which I was
informed my wax
would melt
no one had gone high
around me,
where's the fear
I asked the
Sun. The birds
are out there
in their scattered
cheep. The people
in New York
like a tiny chain
gang are connected
in their
knowing
and their saving
one another. The

morning trucks
growl. Oh

save me from
knowing myself
if inside
I only melt.

AND

when the tiny
plane landed
it sounded
like my camera
rewinding

I thought,
this is
just a
picture

SNAKES

for Kathe Izzo

I was 6 and
I lost my snake.

The table shook
I can do better
than this
and shambled
to the kitchen
to the scene
of the crime

I was green
I put my sneaker
down, little shoe

I felt the cold
metal tap
my calf

moo and everything
began to change.
I am 6
turned into lightning
wrote on the night

At 6, I was feathers
scales, I fell into
the slime of it, lit

You think you are six,
it yelled. I am face

to face with a frog
a woman alone
in bed. The square
of the window
persists. I am 6.

The phone rings
it's my sister
blamm I dropped
a plate. Sorry.

Now the clouds slide
by afraid, awake
my feet are cold
but I'm fearless

I am 6.
Under here
with bottle caps
and stars
adults and low
moans, busses

slamming on brakes
I am 6

the cake is lit
it's round
the children
sing. I will never
return. We are
so small.

My husband turns
his fevered
face. I put
the medicine
down. Click.
I am 6.

The movie rolls on.
Tramping feet,
music blaring
at the end of
the war, I
am frightened
hold my hand

The round face
of the woman
upstairs, moving
the faucets, strips
of vegetable

slithering down,
her reptile child
will never
return. The telephone
rings. It's me.
I'm six.

INFINITY MINI

I was taking
pictures
without
looking
today
look at that
our shadows
without the
determination
the scrunch
of the
photographer.
A woman
passing by
with her
cat
talking softly
to her pussy
who was
once on
a leash.
I don't avoid
a joke
I don't
fight it
the duck
gets moved
by the
wind
all the sounds
and there
are thousands
sound
like laughter.

If you walk
your cat
on the beach
on a leash
you can't be
nervous

two people
push their
canes in the
sand ahhh
he groans
I can feel
that Sun
I can
feel them
now; it's
time to
take a picture
& I aim.

I continue
the earlier
version

hey ducks
I don't
look

There are ripples
going everywhere
the exposed
beach &

I laugh
I laugh at nature

for instance
these twigs
I die

I could run
for some
film

these kooky
sticks

3, 20
could be
in a gallery

tumbling,
barnacles
up to their
necks

the sprig
of seaweed
dangling

I lean
just to put
my butt
in the place
I am

and a man
in a hat
stands
there
& I'm the picture

somebody chase
that cat
a distant
woman
going goddamn

Rosie points
to the
fracas

She's the arrow
my new
"I"

There's
something to see
and there's
something to
smell

Language,
it doesn't
last long

MT. ST. HELENS

Joel Colten
died right
here. He
was a poet.
He visited
me once. In
his car
with a polaroid
camera. I
got it some-
where. Portrait
of Eileen
by Joel Colten
I know I've got
a picture
of him.

And you
can see
the landscape
travelling by
with some
poets in
their 20s
when I knew
Joel Colten
I was
younger then.
it's a
story said
Juliette yah
all that
lava. I don't
think of

him but
I use his
lines all
the time
I had
this poem
on my wall
for a year
see they
get born
on the left
I tell
my class
it's it's
a spine. I mean
Joel Colten's
a snap
of his
nerves
heading right
the infinity
of his line
born, die

every time
the
gesture
is complete
Joel Colten
he died
here.

I don't know
it could be
jets or something
I'm trying
to read
the world
a smokey criss
cross
in the sky
paths
intersect
occasionally

we were
a miracle
once
I'll try

MY HAT

Sometimes
I feel
so sad

I don't
want
to open
the door
& get
out

I want
to stay
in this
special
place
forever
all day
I've looked
at bumpy
pieces of
land & these
are the prettiest
trees echoed
in the waters

which are
bluer the
further I
go. I'm
excited about
getting
to see
you. Your

voice was like
salt in
my life
on the phone.
I could
cry &
the landscape
envelops
me in
mist. It's
astonishing,
handsome
to fly like
a bird in
the pink
& brown
sky. My
heart shoots
ahead.

WEATHER

I had already begun
being a woman who lived
mostly alone, going *huh*
and piping, shuffling
through the rest
of her time. I contain
a running kid, a
green elf. I am
entirely alone. I desire
a certain sports car
a drippy night. Making
hairpin turns
in rome your
face beams
up like a million
jiggling suns.

Do you get
it? Go.
what you
know is
true. I am so
long gone
down my
road.

SYMPATHY

She's rubbing his shoulder
and he's reading about
Western birds. There's a scoop
of light just above my knee

it resembles the world, the one I know
a layer of smoke spread thin, a shelf

my mind returns again &
again to the picture
you gave me. In pain.
I'm holding the receiver
in Denver some woman making
human eyes at me from her
blue seat, but I later
conclude she's crazy

I'm helpless, rushing back to fix the
"h," how can I help you

I think we tried this long enough
our cure
we would save us from everybody
else, we 'got' it,
us

and now we're another falling down car
complaining animal
empty house

you bleeding & expanding
until

the red night itself
is your endless disappointment
in me
who promised so much
on that hill.

O Glory to everybody & everything
that we will fish again & again
& get lucky

BONE

It was raining out tonight
I missed your anywhere
ness
you push someone out of
your life
and you miss them in
the most unexpecting
ways. To come home
& say how are you
each lack each pit
of the rain slowing down outside
reminds me of your missing
warmth, your regularity.
I hated living with you
I had enough
I know you hate me for
having said it with Roses
I can't believe I'm back
in this shitty place
all alone
a dog bone on my desk
everything anywhere it wants
I'd wind up writing to you
like the traffic in
the street

I'd wind up hearing our distant
songs
this morning I wept like a fool
obediently at one of the
little things you sent me,
you meant to make me cry
it's the black coffee
of the morning

I'm lonely in the world
and I can send email, email
email

leave eggs on the plate
there's one
the dog can destroy
the couch
buy another one
I believe in the succession
of values,
sweetness following stuck
play my horn in bed
all alone
dirty, lost & free

THE GUEST

Rilke went
to artist colonies.
My body
has no
friend.
The ocean is many maneuvering
things

A wet
thing to
summon up
the chill
in me

flocks of
breath

the ghostly you
who fluttered
around the
dimpled
flesh of middle
age

then resuming
to be my own
cigarette

and matrimonial
I'm not

pretending
to be

what a blast
of white light
we were

I'll sit closer
to the heat &
my hands
become true

I truly have
given up
on handsome
animal pleased
remembered
the rumpled sheets
I have never
loved anyone
the photograph
that returned
in the mail
the woman laughing
and heaving

Green & lavender
holding a
basket

Couldn't believe
your calendar
your great
train of events
certainly you were
loving someone
going to meet

anyone's
family
the little black key
to Soho Grand
there's a slot
next to my bed
apart from furniture
the spot is me
after we bought
the house
only the lousy
little apartment
had sex

you putting this
silly book
in a nook
like I just
put a stamp
on you & mailed
you to hell
what's it like
there your
radiance pouring
over whatever
the email brings

I hate my
autonomy
cold knuckles

let's face
it Nick
I write shit

and Michael
painting up
in the air
and Marylyn
gravitating
towards Hyannis
my friends
where is our table

Is memory
enough. I've
lost a good word
for nose. And
my face is Helen's,
a part of nature.
This sweet whistle
is a cousin of
the desperate
sound of a storm
at sea.

     My
thigh planted
four feet
from the heat &
the tugging impulse
to be

Overcome in
a hotel in Boston
by terrible
heat.

Susan is
my friend.
You can't go
on your girlfriend's
book tour

What about
menopause

Susan said
I will be in New York
we need a
new population
there
ivy league
girls flooding
the artist colonies

the toilets
broke

putting the final
touches on
your handsewn
manuscript
made out of
your mother's
old clothes

Tim wearing
a woman's
hat that final year
an easter bonnet
really a band

little purple flowers
an old lady's
hat like a rug
with a muscle

I tuck my shirt
and stuffed
it in the nook
with the poet's small
book

Don't you
know that
you're the
horse? Rearing
through your life

I invented
rooms for your
motors, the veins
of the beach
running through
your ears and
your eyes,

       head

I was your
landscape

Here I am
a cold chunk
of marble
pencil-drum

I can go see
Morgan at
the craft fair
bought some
new cups: blue,

Bring me back
that blue cup
that I smashed
on the way
to LA

It fucking spoiled
everything

Whale cup
with a little
spot for a thumb-
print

Oh prove it's morning
not red night
the unforgiven
belt of time
in which
animals feast
on my mind

in which a woman
in Minneapolis
a piece of meat
wrapped in plastic
is dropped
into the refrigeration

unit by many men
with thick arms
who grow old killing
cows and oiling and
adjusting the clocks
that move the animals
to doom and in
our mouths
Some men send their
daughters to college
with pieces of paper
that distantly own
these men &
their work
the insulting
piece of meat
the daughter
carves.

Rear up

The first man that
loved me
sent mail to you.
She said thank
you for the
delivery.
Said stars and the
strangeness
that wood has eyes

that cry for their
missing limbs, I
fear

burial, loss, the
spoiled waters of
love's foiled charge,
my warm flesh
slaps your fevered
white face goodbye.

My body has
no friend.

on my way
2001

HARMONICA

Don't want to put my glasses on
Cause I don't want to see

Don't want to move again
Because I don't want to
Live

Don't want to love again
Because I don't want
To lose

Don't want to eat again
Because I don't want
To be full

Don't want to drink
Again because I don't
Want to feel quenched

Don't want to sleep again
Because I don't want to
Wake up

Don't want to live in the summer
Again because I don't want
To be hot

Don't want you to kiss me again
Because I don't want to be alive

Don't want to see you again
Because I don't want to vanish

Don't want to ride my bike
Because I don't want to
Get there

Don't want to know my family
Anymore because I don't want
To remember me

Don't want to walk my dog
Because I don't want to be out

Don't want to stay in anymore
Because I don't want to be
Alone

Don't want to be tired anymore
Because I don't want to feel old

Don't want to eat candy anymore
Because I don't want to feel sweet

Don't want to talk to my friends anymore
Because I don't want them to know me

Don't want to sing anymore
Because I don't want to hear me.

Don't want to die anymore
Because I don't want to see god.

Don't want to live anymore
Because I don't want to repeat

SCRIBNER'S

There's a little
more going
on here
than preservation

your water
tower against
the sky

your faded
message

two windows
mucking up
the S &
the I

still I know
it was 43rd St.
where I
badly slept
with you

my memory:
I was
perfect then

there's more
than that
that's going
on

just breathing
is rotting
everything

is burning
I'm probably
madly
in love with
you

but it's her
I'm leaving
tonight or
me & my
lousy lies

so lolling
around in
another
lost home
with your
camera

checking perfection
before you
got film &
now I don't
want those
damn pictures

the teletubby
transfixed
nailed to
some scaffolding
on 42nd St.

the poking tower
over the

dirty parking
lot wall

with the
yellow stripe

that's right
I'm not
Mr. Teletubby

it was sad
every time
we took
a picture

this is a relationship
click
this is a relationship

if my cover
is an illustration
of me &
so is my
writing an
observation
of truth

not it
fucking scaffolding
right,
fucking burning

alive
Spring is so

perfect tonight
because outside
in the real
house the
birds are
shamefully true
hopping under
the hokey
sidewalk
furniture shitty
captured flowers
looking droopy

Rosie just
wants to
put her belly
on some cool
cement. Does.

I do this.
Appear to
be a bum
in my hiking
boots & hairy
legs I'm no
longer a dyke
just a man

hello little
bird.

Sorry, Tree
2007

NO REWRITING

nobody's going to come in
and take my cup of money

sometimes the only no I have
is to reverse things

I agree. It's a good place to shit.

This morning it was summer
while I stayed in
I watched spring fade
I went out in chill fall
and walked my dog
in winters rectangles of trash
striking our face
the wind turning flags and banners
into danger
man the wind was big
in this fragmented
city

I want to be a part of something bigger than myself
not the university of california but it's a start
my dad was a gorilla

who did you think I would be

how do you spell univercity
it always looks cilly

I will think
I will read

I will wake up loving you and when I come home
I will love you.
Look I bought tickets for the movies for tomorrow night
I will buy you a hot dog then you know what

They didn't know I was so great
it was humbling
now it is fine

I sent her this email about the big awards
the paranoia I feel about all the award
winners
now I'm like king of the losers again
I said king king king

it's like genitals
I want to show you all these tiny parts

but I'm public public public

I went to the University of Massachusetts
and for all these years the city of New
York has given me a rent stabilization
grant

and now California golden state opens her
arms to us

come to mama

I wrote this poem twenty-four years ago
but nobody saw it yet
so I'm safe

she said you are such a good boy

that morning I had just moved my car
today on the blue paper the hell's angels flag is
rolled like toilet paper, just a thin stream
of tattered flag thanks to the accident
of weather last night's wind

and I got back in bed and she called
I think the bridges will be closed

and everyone was screaming on the roof
there's another one
no she said I'm watching teevee
so I brought her up to the roof with me
and all my neighbors standing up there the whole block
like history and it flaming

and I met the poet Jason from the building next door
they've hit the pentagon someone yelled
and I went down to get some coffee
and when I came back one was down
wow I said to Jason
had I let go of you yet I can't remember
I went back to get some more
and none were left

I drink a lot less coffee now and I can sleep at night
but who could miss the flag like fourth of july
forever when they move the car
I think of it so much
when I ride over the Manhattan Bridge
on my bike or my car
when else do I look up
I never used to notice the towers

riding around Berlin This used to be a wall neighborhood
the wall was here, here, here
god they're haunted I thought
but where was it did I ever know
I just thought of it as 70s
and suppose it would've been nice to be a poet in residence
another grant I never got around to sending in

it was never out my window but I see it out there now

last night I thought about tripping
and the way the fags had yellow canvas deck chairs
and it was labor day and everyone was gone

it wasn't enough to sit on their furniture
at their little round table with the umbrella

we had this skid on the other side of the roof
they called it the dyke deck
and I remember lying there with our shirts off
so early in the morning
getting more and more sweet quarts of bud
writing with a soft pen
into the cheep industrial wood

more rebop

we thought fuck them
and threw the yellow deck chairs into the trees in the yard
they just hung there and we laughed and laughed
woke up thought oh no
there was a moment when they thought about evicting us
all the men

even the super Bill
who had some kind of anal cancer
an old marine who kept painting the foyer
you called it
the building's butt-hole

yellow and green
tan then brown
by the time he painted it horrible shiny silver
so bad when I was drunk
I thought what a goner
and yep he was dead soon

speaking of smells or halls tubes for living through

I think of Belansky:

Little Girl

mainly I think you just have to take the loss into account
I don't care if you get it

Little Girl

holes in my memory

sticking my hands in my jeans
jackets
which ones have the torn pockets
I repaired
and where do I put my keys
now
which pants am I in
do I remember them?

the bread must be saved
wrapped, protected
from age
because I am poor

and how am I to dress my flesh
if I'm not poor
anymore

how can I protect me from rotting
how can I allow

buy a new loaf everyday
throw it away
wildly fresh

Belansky who stunk
who never went out
hermit with a beard
and the stink poured when he opened
his door

little girl
go to the store for me
to buy baloney
and raisin bread
and two quarts of milk
for years
and keep the change

little girl

I'm 28
35
forty even forty
while he was still alive
some days walking really
slow past his door
I even knocked
I was so broke
I needed his forty cents

the day his stinky apartment was empty
now for years
the clean old man his brother
where were you all this time
when your brother had a beard
came to New York for something
grew inside here

FOR JORDANA

I really do feel like
I am in some French
movie,
blam putting
down a general
cup of tea. The
lights are thus
and I squiggling
then returning
to my work
quietly squeezed
through the
day that's captured
some way
separately
not the squares
of the cinema
but envelopes
of affection

spea
spep
spe

separation

I think writing
is desire
not a form
of it. It's feeling
into space,
tucked into
language
slipped

into time,
opened,
felt. All this
as a matter

of course
of course

yet being
here somehow,
open

EACH DEFEAT

Please! Keep
reading me
Blake
because you're going to make
me the greatest
poet of
all time

Keep smoothing
the stones in the
driveway
let me fry an egg
on your ass
& I'll pick up
the mail.

I feel your
absence in
the morning
& imagine your
instant mouth
let me move
in with you—
Travelling
wrapping your limbs
on my back
I grow man woman
Child
I see wild wild wild

Keep letting the
day be massive
Unlicensed
Oh please have
my child
    I'm a little
    controlling
    Prose has some
    Magic. Morgan

had a
whore in
her lap. You
Big fisherman
I love my
Friends.

I want to lean
my everything
with you
make home for your hubris
I want to read the words you circld over and over again
A slow skunk walking across the road
Yellow, just kind
of pausing
picked up the warm
laundry. I just saw a coyote
tippy tippy tippy
I didn't tell you about the creature with hair
long hair, it was hit by cars on the highway
Again and again. It had long grey hair
It must've been a dog; it could've been
Ours. Everyone loses their friends.

I couldn't tell anyone about this sight.
Each defeat
Is sweet.

UNNAMED NEW YORK

here in the beautiful
heat
digging & digging for
you
in your wide & wonderful
pause
day subway
de doggie
I was trying
to say it
writes
in bites
citizen aged local literary
queer cocksucking shop-
ping pussy
manifesting not
will Arnold win
if you enjoyed
smoking in bars
study French expressionism
employ your
loss
buy a car
take a course
make a college
buy something old
again & again
& again
the sneaker
swings
I like it here:

it's orange
& my hands are free.

The new book
was composed by picking shit
out of a wave.
Wherever they said vague
I thought vague

I couldn't help laughing
standing at the bottom
of my pit.
I thought Mark Twain was
here in the
crater of a giant
tomato
big artists like error.
The tomato
Missed.
Being intended
to hit god
it hit his mother
I speak for
her.

APRIL 5

you realize you have no
pants on as you're
walking down to the
pool
I have no pants on I
say
in this very unattractive
poem.
Your hair is wetly matting
your pubic bone & upper
thighs. I have to
get something
I tell my companion
and look there are
dogs
maybe this was just
before
as I'm playing over the
keys
of my fading dream.
One dog's really nice
little
the other dog poised
on a landing is bigger
& I get mad.
This one is for you.
I'm turning wildly
looking for newspaper
I realize I'm in
one of those dreams.
We've just showered
everything's perfect
when I say let's
go to the pool

and you agree
the warm pool
in this mysterious
public country
that has no head
no future. I have
no pen I'm
in bed
the shame of nakedness
how mad the dogs
made me, the
world is inside out
sounds on the street
(now gone)
in my new neighborhood
coming into sight
as the headless
country full of meaning
and you were there
with me
in my problem

always naked
fading
truth

THAT COUNTRY

I've just
never known
what
to call
that country.
If I say
England
I don't think

I sound so
smart. I keep
tripping up
on their language which is English
so shouldn't their
country be the
same. Britain seems wrong,
does anyone
go to Britain?
People go to London
that's where they go.
There's really no country at all
just a city
huge, old
haven't been there for a while.
& UK is just a concept
a fashion statement
an economy
it seems you could have
a relationship
with that
but you wouldn't *go* there
you would allude.
Though, it includes everything,

doesn't it: the UK.
Ireland, Scotland,
England, all of it.
England is right

in there, but no place
else, which is why
I never say it.
But what about the
language they speak.
English. My penmanship
sharpens up. I go to
        school.
Slowly the words appear
on a line. Could I
write in that language
Think in it
Do I
am I missing something.
I really think a lot:
The second l in really
staggered into a y
the letters got
drunk. I wanted
to fuck up this
language & blame
its nameless
homeland:
the victors got drunk
they came & came
the words were never
the same again
in the last century
it came to us

to speak American
which means
to speak
where you land
which means
nothing now.
Not proud
but invasive.
Not the language
not the place
not them
not us
neither an island
nor a continent
nor a world
a spin without
a home.
An edgy
feeling. A coin
on its
side
speaking up

I'M MOVED

a squiggle of a river
becomes a road
in a play a boy
might walk
around a lot
and a woman
might be still.
Something in the water
might look like
brains
when the boy's
just sitting
there being
young; day
the moment might oc-
cur in memory
sentiment
I know musicians
know certain
chords do this
or that
we're a bunch
of turtles
when it comes
to feelings
the woman
is still and the
world around
her darkens
and we get
it—just
before the
boy started
walking. I wish the playwright

was brave.
to stay in that
corny suggestion
darkness
means
sadness
means time.
It's just our
burning star
and our
blue dirt
turning in its circle
a stand-in
for emotion
for scientists: you.
Who promised
to bring her
binoculars
somewhere, now here, to this grand
play. Just to
discover
art makes
me look
long & hard.
Why is light
so damn emotional
if it's just
a burning star.
This toe,
an inch

SAN DIEGO POEM

the jacarandas turn on like lights
city heights is in fact beautiful
guided by voices
disturbs me however
I will get to the 15
going north to Adams
to return disc 2
of Brazil
I hated it when it came out
the same
thing I always hate
dirty like Kienholzes
like dirty technology
the midwest
which is like London
somehow greasy
who gets British humor
I can't
I think of my dad
who purportedly liked
sex so much
in fact sex in this
town
did he ever know
his little kid would
teach college
here pull over under
purple trees
to think about him

& the urge

CIGARETTE GIRL

a long rain
drop more
of a tear
fell from
an awning or a nail
shit the top
of a roof
and hit my neck
inside my
coat
I don't know
how it got
in so perfectly
& struck
my flesh
my warm
white neck
on a rainy
night in
winter
I almost
said this to you

she wanting
to move on
if I spoke
another language
I'd break into
it now
there's nothing
lonelier
than a lonely
American
my limits

contract &
expand

I grab the white
handle of
my speech
like it's an
umbrella
and I shake
it free
of words
empty American
balloon
holy smoke

looking out
at the
street
it's nothing
to know
you, puff

TO HELL

for J.

I'm not sure who I walk with in America today.

I miss you, my imagined accomplice, while we're
      moving among men

One man stands up and says his daughter's gay

Like we didn't know that she says, he thinks it's so great

We can't think it's so wonderful, being lied to for years

We've accomplished bright cynicism, then struggle for love

We flounder, we fail, the elephant eliminates the con-
      fusions of love.

Love probably didn't need a war, couldn't eat, is rolling
      on waves today

The city is emptying. The elephants have been planning
      their party for years.

I'm heading into it. New York my home bursting with men.

Conservative women, heading downtown to see a cross made
      of girders: "Great!"

Jesus marked this city, threw planes at it, face it those
      pilots were gay

We're gonna make a constitutional amendment against em
      for being gay.

Gay to hit buildings, to want to meet in great numbers,
       being no one Love

Moving like an angry sunflower, wanting bandages, space,
       something great

I want to live here feeling celebrated for breathing open
       today.

I want to show you complicated dyke love, construct a poem
       about women and men

In my country there's a basic responsibility to struggle
       and not for years.

To walk away, to turn around seeing you and progress and be
       loving your smile for years

Sometimes I think there's complication with men but I'm
       probably gay

Gay to be glad to keep expressing and knowing the im-
       possible hopes of women and men

I would want to learn more, be firmer, open up,
       revolutionize love streaming

A house on a hill is pretty but there's something
       rhapsodically fine today

Stay here while the American ship is moving and rocking,
       vincible, great.

My moment alone in front of everyone is hopelessly great

I don't have to wonder where I'm going this time or this
        year

I don't have to wonder whose group I'm in today.

Certainly the people who always think the public problem is
        theirs are gay

When the moment comes to move like trees to free the city I
        love

I don't know John Kerry and we can name that feeling Bud-
        dhist for the next four years

The pond reflects the sky, if the highway curls it's gay.

A public moment, a political moment is what's possible
        today

We trust more than men, something's eating our years

The uneven horizon's great and of course she's gay

The buildings are falling in love, and we opened its eye
        today

Snowflake / different streets
2012

TRANSITIONS

for Rocco

sometimes
I'm driving
and I pressed
the button
to see who
called &
suddenly I'm
taking pictures.
Big dark
ones. He says
it's not about
where you sit
to make a
film
but I wasn't
taking a
picture
I was driving
it's black &

there's all
these lights
I'm strong
it's night
& I've

driven very
far

I keep hearing
the music

of the weekend
he says
it's not about
whether she & I
resume
it's how it goes
on
with me.

In my car
so long ago
I loved someone
who read me a poem
on the phone
about the car
of the day

you mean the
one I'm driving

and the fact that
she left it
on the phone
and that was new

she said I was overreacting
and that was too much
and we sent our messages
in light
and ack she hated
trees
I thought she's so
young cause
I like nature

now and her trunk
wrapped around
me one day
he licks my
arm my boy
& driving home I thought
if he dies
I will see his paw
in the sky
I am seeing it now
and she's always
home
going hwuh
and she said
I love our little
meeting I said

little

don't denigrate
my need to support

my need to say
that you *can*

I'm glad I'm
home   it's wide
out there
we spoke about scaf-
folding
him fitting the
frame to the
eye
she's grown

I wanted to say
we laughed about
tang
and later on the
toilet
thought
about tango
and joan
L Tango Larkin
what's not technology
what's not seeing
an arm to say
I hold the
line   I hold
the day
I watch the snowflake
melting

SNOWFLAKE

There's no female
in my position

There's no man

wow
there's a raccoon
on the tail
of the plane
and there's
no one

seeing that now
but me

and there's no one close
enough right
in here
to see the
further
drawing
stripes or buildings
the bricks
of the world
I wonder
what I'll say about Sadie
and I wonder
if they are still
living in that
state
and if they hate
me for moving
her furniture

out and putting
it in storage

I walked past that restaurant
where I was so mad
I could have broke
the glass
I'm the only one in the mood to remember
this me living

who threw
a snowball
against the
glass
and scared
me in my seat
so hot
with rage
why am I dry
freezing
I want to go
home

I saw a rose
in the heart
of the
year two thousand one
everything
turning
rose
dog head
a wheel of
love
but I was so mad

I locked it
up and took
the key and lived
for that moment
snowflake
I wasn't there
not even me
when she put
in the key
and it wouldn't
turn

D.H.

Politically speaking
look at this
a word at a time
on my knee
looking forward to a picnic
with my friends
in the afternoon
in their car
but no the climate is such
that I never
arrive
stayed on the stair
master
one more time
I'm depressed
all my life
enraged the man behind
me as we plow
into the brite grey light
it's evening here
bright as a flea
as I enter the history
of intellectuals
who escaped *that*
to land in
this eternal
sun
burning what's left
of the earth
never meeting
anyone

CHOKE

Of all the ways of forgetting
not turning the pilot on is not
                  the worst

The house is intact
you are floating
in time
buckets of it streaming through
              the windows

youth turned it up I think
or on & fell asleep

Remembering to do.
You are too intact
the dappled sunlight on the lawn
or pots of darkness
like salt instead of depths

Still once I turned it up
the popping commenced
like applause for the present
tense
the site of my sway

Larry's new car is wide & safe
a woman's voice conducts
us left & right
she's crazy he laughs
again & again

my shrink said buy it now
about the car

I told him about my phenomenal streak
of winning & when the stakes
rose I began to bid low &
not at all
I could have won; you choked
he said.

Woof. To not choke
is I suppose to experience
to hold it in & go forth
though you need the heat

The sun had not done more
suddenly for a while

it's like we took off our skin
and said it is hot.
It's like we sold our skin
& said where did everyone go?

when the weather's too hot for comfort
& we can't have ice cream cones
it ain't no sin
to take off your skin
& dance around in your bones

CAESAREAN TOOTHBRUSH

for Alice

I left it outside
for a yuk
for those that we know
who may never come
in
but riding by they'll
know what I'm
doing. They will know
I'm okay.
It's what we want
to know about
everything. We don't
want to get sprayed
by it. More than
once it's been
suggested to me
that if I looked
more closely
I'd see that it's
normal. So I live
with weird but
familiar. To traffic
it looks okay.
My jokes are mostly
travelers' jokes
I go to unusual lengths
to get what most
people get. In my defense
I like it hard.
My cat's name is Marco
Polo. His severe profile

gazing into the
dead end
of the apartment.
Hey that's not
going out.
That end goes
out. To him I just
become invisible
for a while
& to me that's
just my life.
This is being his secretary.
Worrying about how
he'll be when
he'll be anything.
Worry about yourself,
Eileen. Stabbing
things. I just did
do it for a very
long time.
In that motion
in that soothing
motion.

The cat is in
the bag
I leave the bag where
it is
so the cat can get
in it and dream
for a very long
time
while the rest
of my building
purrs

he slipped his head
into the bag's
handles & gently
sniffs it

well then money
well then love

YOUR NAME

It's very hard
to hunt
from indoors
I'll say that for
you. And
text is
at best
an attenuated
warning
sound has
a range
of many desires
not just map.
I subscribe
to the grandpa
bunny bunny school
of theory
I mean genesis
to write
is a form
of accounting
& approximate
promise
in the sunny
mouth of
time. A horny
bet. Or else
hunters
lolling around the fire
what did you
get. How can
we avoid it.
This "making
a speech." Long limbed

& maybe
in July. Aren't
we lucky to have
captured each
other in this
hideous neon light.

MITTEN

It's beautiful. I mean
it's beautiful *here*
but the thing
is it is beautiful.
The peach sky is beautiful
and black outlines
of the branches
and the leaves
look I even
hesitate but it doesn't
matter if it all comes
at once or breaks
down slow. Catch this
honking or the rumbling
of the world. Last
night in "Different
Streets" which I didn't
bother to write I made
the point that the two places
are connected and it's great
where you are too
and boom boom rumble
all the places are connected
thus the endless
beauty. And I have been
beaten & suffered and you
have too. Whoop whoop
listen to that someone
getting arrested. Someone
caught, someone's heart
just stopped. Someone
else holding the bag.
I wrote something else
about the day holding me

and me holding you. A car
passes like a big breath.
It's what I've got: all these
things and I hand them
to you like sex in the city.
My ideal. Our endless
sound. Our connection.
Listen to *all* your voices now.

HI

for Steve Carey

You made me smell.
I didn't smell at
all before I met you
smells are pouring out of
my clothes, feet, my
socks my hair
this is gross
you've made me monstrous
and I love it
I knew a man who laughed
at himself
for being this way
stinking of love
it was what he was
a stinking factory of his love
lying there all day
going out to get a smoke
I'm the east coast version
of that
since I met you
since the era of my famous
resistance to you ended
it began like the wind
I am a window to the world
the mailman can see me
he waves; children out there playing
it's even this way when I'm out
there
except when I hold your hand
I want it; to be this exception
I've become

not a woman or a man
The heart pumps
the man is dead and it's
spring
it's a smelly season
don't you think
the earth knows
the bugs are beginning to look
around
you're throwing your mother's
old stuff out
your friends are beginning
to understand
I want to show
mine something different
the ripples I've become
I'm influence
the way language changes
and rocks heal & burn
meat stretches
your little round animal
face keeps coming around
the corner but
oh no now you're coming down
I'm looking up

THE WEATHER

for Alan, Monica & Frances

For the most
compelling
birthday party I'd
been to in
a while
I bought three
cards.

Thinking that
I heard a wet
and sparkling
sound three pipes
spurting
water standing in the
park quite
near to the corner
I meet you on
I go past.
I don't know what
tonight will de-
liver
the teeshirt

you'll wear
an attachment
I'm proud
of not knowing
you again
like that water
I've lived here
for a while.

What do you think
I should say
in these
cards?

I'm as excited
about this moment
as I was in the
beginning
I keep seeing
women in the street
who resemble
my mother her
wide Christian
face. Is it an abomination
to put that
in a poem to
my lover
not so much to
you as with
you in it
in the same world
of the card
the train-ride into
Brooklyn
cars turning
skateboard
splash
hard the plastic
of the wrong side
hitting the
pavement. All you
see are cops

cars & their
vans prowling
like a city
full of
meth. Or whole
middle of a
country
like a split.

Every woman your
age
cute. Every woman
my age
wounded &
glisten.

SMILE

It's just not as much fun without a good
light and a sharp knife
I mean leaning into the peach of
it. People find the time
to get theirs sharpened or use yours.
That drip in the kitchen is like
someone I know. Today's cold
is like an affirmation of the purchase
of yesterday's new shirt. I knew the cold
would come some time but today.
I'm wearing that drip most of all.
My half-made meal and even the space
that surrounds the incredible possibility
of hunger on and on like my favorite man
Frankenstein. The drip has tones.
A relationship with the holding
bowl that is only holding water.
All these rhymes all the time. I used to
think Mark Wahlberg was family.
So was Tim but close to his death
he told me he was adopted. Every
time he smiled he thought Eileen
is a fool. Or that's what love looks
like. If I woke and my master was horrified
I would go out into the world with this
enormous hurt. And I have carried mine
for so long I now know it's nothing special.
It's just the fall and the sound of her sirens. It's the agony
of being human. Not a dog who dies maybe six
times in the lives of her masters. Everyone's phony
and made up. Everyone's a monster like me.
Now I know everyone.

THE PERFECT FACELESS FISH

It is a miracle
that I should speak
to delight you.
I feel like a flag
more or less
but music is my breeze
I have many friends
rest assured.
You have given me
my water
and for this I must
thank you. You have
been described
as elegant in your time
and it is long
the road to go
I am honored to accompany
you. A picture
is simply what I am
an old crease
a perfect book
you will miss me
in your sterile anticipation
of something to hang
this picture on. I come
& go. An edible saint.
But if you feast
on me you will be hungry.
I know your intelligence
carnal somehow
and I began to speak
when you began to want
me. Please don't interrupt
I cross my legs

I flood the darkened
rooms of art

for a while.
And frankly that moment
is gone.
We could only talk through
our eyes and now
that is gone. But this
is deeper than
the marrow
we don't need rods cones
those sanskrit piles of things
I am seeing through a stain
right now
in your love
I am swimming for years.
In a sudden absence
of trouble in a deftly
handled conversation
I, a luminous fish
felt in this spectacle of impossibility
a fragrant graze upon the
world
an intermittent twitch,

whisper. If I had hands
I would touch everyone
I vanish in the green
of the background
that goes on and on
made by those who recognize
it that way
there is always something better

to do
I live in a terminal
and so do you
listen we are trying to end everything
by this enormous silence
brief
but it was the old thing
so it shall be very loud
very loutish in the squabbles we
have about right & wrong
& where the flagpole is and
do we ever
will we ever have enough
space to play the game
I am deeply knowing you
and feel you have chosen
me for this conversation
before it's cooked
before anything is prepared
anything at all
the lesser details never mind
the first exquisite choice
that brought me into being
this conversation
a fishy birth
I've had you in my pocket
it's all that I know
but a knowing that is useless
without this acknowledgment
in a many chambered room
ew
is that what you said
enormous darkly I accept it
I flow around and fold

into everything your comic
desultory contempt
which I'm beginning to see
functions as glue
for you
the prettiness for me is
the opening city
and moving through it with you
the young old fold
around your mouth
seismic
trust that
I am gold in the reconciliation
gold in the anticipation
paradise great ambiance
what's available
is not of any use to
what is me today
a stoic longing symbol of
studying peace
in outlandish quarters
your long room in the night
your whole long body
which is faceless too
to acquire your trust is of
utmost importance to me
I am foolish I talking fish
the time is here for me
to make promises to
you that is sometimes standing
in a bakery
laughing becomes a professional
wife with empty folders
and I see the muscle

embedded the one
that can't be removed
in the beloved text that is
offered
a torso sized drink to me
each time I break the surface
turn around
bubbles cascading from
the incommensurate
path of my tale, tentacle
limbs
you make me enough
so I hold a cup
gasping with laughter
in the teeshirts covered with
arcane scribbles
carry the message
awkward grins and phones to
their ears
yours are wired to everything
there is
you're an impossible telephone
I lift my head for the
last sip of your
ew
a lamb leaps over the fins
the arms I would
have we would hold
each other in
I am waiting. No difficulty
with gold. As I told
your mother I have
obtained access
to an uncontrolled intimacy

fear not
certainly I did not phrase it
that like
but I met her in
the most advanced
communication terrain
and exchanged
messages concerning our
difficulties with god
and man
I am beginning to know
I am gold a transforming
ship
the clipped end of an
utterance I was saving
for you when I saw your

swinging light
the door approach
and everything moves
   close

MY BOX

in terms of
design one
box is colored
orange

the one you wanted
always is and
sits in the bathroom
of anyone's
house cause
that's what
she wants
it's choosing
that wakes things
up

I wondered how
long all
that I needed and encountered
here
would come like a wave
not the shake
but the after
effects
and this box
did say
there was a way
to see this
thing
a-
lone

July called
it calculus

what is
comes in boxes
what is not
comes in waves
the dots
between

mountains
surround us
and I say
they are more
marvelous than
the sea

way overhead

I like flying over
them too
thinking
that is home
these crazy bumps
when we drive
into them
tomorrow
it won't be bam
it means up
swirling on the
edge of a
cup and if you
don't watch
me like a
hawk I won't
be scared
I want to be

loved like
a sunbeam
that is
it comes
across the room
or the ocean
you know the
way I drive
I want to lift
your fear
like a bonnet
and kiss
your living
face. Here
this is
mine. Don't
misunderstand
me.

epilogue

ANONYMOUS

(Mic Check!)

NO I'M THE POET

NO YOU'RE THE POET

NO HE'S THE POET

NO THEY'RE THE POET

NO SHE'S THE POET

NO THAT'S THE POET

NO THIS IS THE POET

NO I'M THE POET

(Repeat)

TWICE

A friend of mine, Dana, was prowling around in the electronic proof of a journal we both are in, *Maggy,* edited by another poet friend Adam, and Dana found my poem "What Tree Am I Waiting"* which I will include here. Now? Well, sure.

WHAT TREE AM I WAITING

That whole part of the world
where I won't go any-
more
that whole separation
that I won't feel
high in this house
in this hemisphere
in this artificial light
that is artificial
in the earliest morning; dark
in pages and pens
in an unfamiliar bed
in the foot curl
furniture
each rumble
when morning comes
and it's still morning
and it's still night
I married a dead girl
we were born in her
bloom
remember that fat bumblebee

---

* Both this poem and "And Then The Weather Arrives" appear earlier in this book so I guess you'll be reading them twice.

landed on a lamp
I opened the doors
and I forgot and the house
got colder and colder
where is this house
the seam between boards
merely gains my attention
it's dark and thin
I monitor each situation
my bladder growing full
climb down climb up
what tree am I waiting
my whole life in weather
waiting for my raft
I'll fly to another island
I'll take a train
already I know
it will hurt
this is the hurt country
I came here
to hold the hurt like a bird
like a tree
traffic has rings
we watch it whirl around
damaging our night
great continents hold
the feelings and the ages
what is mine
going blind
great masses of them
not going home
the country drew a line
because of memory
one said
I feel my heart race ahead
in eternity there is this ache
there is this wakefulness

Dana wrote me because he was very excited about this poem. He said he was "getting pee-shy (ha ha) about *my own thing*" (which was a joke since his describes among other things taking a piss and he wonderfully calls his own dick "the disaster of the world"). His explanation of why my poem was important to him was like balm to my ears. He wrote:

> To hear someone arrive with that purpose & then put it right there, getting out of the way of everything else to get it right to the top of the thought & the poem. That's the best stuff in the world to me, that sound. It seems harder than ever to do, or I'm confused right now somehow, regardless, it just tolled in the room for me.

This was huge praise from someone whose work I currently adore. I was pee-shy too about my own poem in particular because it was so emotional. How will it be received. Dana did refer to his own piece in *Maggy* as "a poem" which intrigued me cause it looked like prose. It's prose in a world in which I've never really noticed whether people describe Bernadette Mayer's influential early works "Moving" and "Memory" as poems or prose. Didn't she call it writing. I mean I think even for Lydia Davis genre is like gender in the poetry world. I'm remembering Amber Hollibaugh explaining gender this way once. It's not what you're doing, it's who you think you are when you're doing what you're doing. So prose writers in the poetry world always felt less like prose writers to us, more like fellow travellers and someone like Bernadette *was* probably writing poems that looked like prose, or like Lydia, prose in the poetry world which for a while at least adds up to the same thing. She was a fellow traveller for a time, and still is, truly, though she's also everyone's now. John Ashbery's greatest book I think is *Three Poems* which certainly looks like prose. So if Dana Ward wants to call his prosey looking stuff a poem it probably has more to do with how he feels about the work. Or *whose* he thinks it is. When I read it, it's mine for sure. I nipped off to his page in *Maggy* right after I read his email to see what he had in there. His piece with the pissing scene was indeed the one he had emailed to me last summer both as part of an extended hello and a particular greeting because his piece was dedicated to Maggie Nelson who he had just met up at Bard where they were both visiting/teaching. Maggie is one of my favorite people (and writers) in the world, and I think my name came up while they were talking and all of this triggered Dana's sending me the piece because he knew I loved Maggie and now he did too. And I mention both of them because if there are two youngish—they might be in their early forties which is by now young to me, being 64 (will you still need me, will you still feed me . . . *No!* was the answer but we haven't gotten there yet)—if there are two people whose work *everyone* likes, it is them. Maggie is also a poet who writes loose, splashing (or maybe slashing) speculative prose and though very different writers (Maggie's more on the balls of her feet, and Dana's loopy warm and risk-taking) they kind of describe a moment in writing in which a lot of things that people like are beginning to need to happen in the *same* pieces of writing and those things may be gossip, theory, sexual description, or simply an implication that *it's* there or just happened (art) but what's great is that while the most feeling-oriented scholars have been calling for this collusion for a while it's in the hands and minds and on the computers of poets that all this continental shift is truly happening. Poetry is the new space of possibility and everyone knows it. Maggie and Dana are two charismatic (and interestingly, both married) wanderers who are working the line between worlds while enjoying the road and packing light. (I think part of the method of their madness is security.)

One thing I want to say also at this moment is that everything I'm describing so far has happened on my computer. Or in it. Dana wrote me, and he had visited my poem on his computer. I visited his; I remembered encountering his last summer in Italy I think and I wrote him back and *then* I look at the letter from the Liverpool Biennial* and then I look at Dana's email again and then I find a couple of poems on my computer and I begin.

---

* This essay you're reading is a response to an invitation from the 2014 Liverpool Biennial for some writing that reflected on or delivered a variety of things including an explanation of "how you deal with the connections between your memories, history of poetry and writing, through events of your own life."

So I wrote Dana back last night and started to talk about my poem. I don't want to say what I said back to him. I'll try and remember what I meant. I wrote my poem last fall. I had been with my girlfriend in Italy last summer and then she went back to New York and then I variously travelled to Lithuania, then Istanbul and I called and wrote her from these places and finally I arrived in Ireland where I was to spend the fall. I went to Dublin, well Dun Laoghaire specifically where my friends Ali & Kathleen live and then we went for a trip down to West Cork and we took ferries to islands and saw two versions of the same play. In one version because we were late we had to stand ears pressed to the wooden door of the community center under the deep blue sky and listen to Carmel's play being performed inside. It was a one-woman show in a small space and we would have entered right in front of the actress which just wasn't possible. The next night we were with the playwright herself, Carmel Winters, who was Ali and Kathleen's friend and now mine. Her actress had to go to a wedding that night so Carmel decided she would do it herself which she did in another small community theater on Sherkin Island. We had been feeling her anxiety all day and I was truly nervous for her but she was tremendous—even bravely donning the same red running outfit as the actress. It was a dramatization of a film she had earlier produced called *Snap* which was about sexual abuse. Pretty riveting and smart. When the writer performs her own text you can really feel what it means. The timing of the thinking is there. I really don't understand acting at all.

I left Kathleen and Ali in a couple of days when they drove me up to Annaghmakerrig, otherwise known as the Tyrone Guthrie Centre. Tyrone Guthrie was queer I learned. And so was his wife. It was a lush retreat with mainly Irish artists. The first night there was tough, since the acoustics in the dining room were not so great and everyone had different Irish accents and everyone spoke very quickly and spoke even faster when they got to the end which was invariably a joke which I didn't get since I didn't know what that *word* was.

On the second night we all took a walk around the lake and just as we were approaching the house to hear some music my cellphone rang. It was my girlfriend. I explained that it wasn't such a good time and she said I think we better speak now. She quickly explained that her playwright friend, Adam, who she had been hanging around with in the month since we'd been apart was now her lover. I told her that maybe it was a good thing which she seemed almost angry to hear but I had this sort of cool elevated even relieved feeling. I had been sensing that something was wrong in the couple of weeks before, our calls getting shorter and shorter and I had even pushed her once about whether she still *loved* me her behavior was so odd and she sort of slid away from my question and didn't answer.

So this was the end of my relationship of four years. I sat in the music room with the other artists that night and was serenaded by a variety of songs that seemed consciously chosen to quell and palp my scrambling soul. Love . . . Love will tear us apart . . ." Peter sang, at which point I heaved myself out of the room, sobbing at last. I think.

I mean it was a strange break up. Does it ever happen by mistake. I think we were meant to break up about now but no one could see the way. She found it. I certainly loved her but I'm old enough to think about that (in some ways) well, so what. There's something else about whether it works which kind of means besides loving, can you stand it. I couldn't. But then I could.

By October I was living in Belfast. I promise you I didn't tell Dana all this. I was living in a little gatehouse to an estate that was no longer there. Instead it was a gatehouse surrounded by streets and streets of similar brick houses and there was a leisure center down the hill where I worked out and a giant Iceland where I bought my food. I had two wood burning stoves and it was already cold and very wet. I was working on a book.

There was a couch that turned into a bed and in the largest room in the little gatehouse there was a giant loft bed and there I lay nightly in hell. I couldn't sleep. And I couldn't stop thinking about my girlfriend and that man, and I thought about how I wished I had broken up with her last summer or the spring that had just passed and then I thought about her with that man. And I had even been betrayed before by a girlfriend with a man named Adam. I felt biblical. Who was I. There is a point in suffering and I mean suffering as a repetition. When you can't sleep or you fall into that bouncy medium stage where the softening of sleep is beginning to occur and then the forbidden thought sneaks in like a tiny seed that bursts into flame but white flame and the blaze feels like day has bombarded the inside of your self, all light dripping down all the windows of your heart and your mind and you look at the ceiling and you look at the tops of the windows bluing across from you and you wonder where in hell are you. Your body goes surge, surge, energy pouring wrongly into all your muscles and joints. You are one hundred percent alive. Wrongly. You are so filled with energy and you'd like to kill and you don't want to kill yourself. You don't really want to kill anyone. It becomes wordless. It's not even late. It's so so early like about seven am, or two am. Who knows what time it is. Something happens at this point. What I did tell Dana is that the thing that's so funny about being a poet is that you write *sorts* of poems. You return to sorts of poems which are sorts of energy. Each poem that really happens and by that I mean one that was conjured in a state that managed to find its own rhythm in something deeply anonymous about the self. I think being a poet or a writer you've spent so much of your time processing, consuming, really creating an alternative self that is entirely composed of language so that there are precise speeds or toxins or organs in it that work in concert with the state that you are in and can only neutralize your own pain by vanishing into a song composed of exactly that timbre, or something. I don't know what it is. It's just that I've vanished into kind of a not trance but dictation that utterly resembled the circumstances I found myself in but by enumerating them I evacuated even from my own pain and wasn't so much out of my body but in it in some other way, deciphering the details around me like a breathing tapestry.

I wanted to say to Dana I wrote that one before. Not the poem but the sort of poem. Tonight I was talking on the phone to Adam, and not the playwright Adam who poached my girl but Adam Fitzgerald, a poet, and a confidant, a new dear friend and the publisher of *Maggy*. Which is not named after Maggie Nelson but nothing feels coincidental, but more incidental. I just wrote him to ask what *Maggy* means. I was telling him I had been in this exact state another time and it really . . . not so much *felt* the same but was made the same. Of the same light. I was having my affair with Bernadette Mayer. *You had an affair with Bernadette Mayer.* Yes, and her husband. *When was this.* 1981. I was a young drunk. Well not so young. Kind of the same age my girlfriend was if you believe in karma. And I don't. *No I don't either.* It went on for about five months. We weren't friends before and we weren't friends after. She's tough. I was in love with her, her husband was in love with me. It kind of ended because she was jealous that he was in love with me. I don't want him. I wanted her. It was absurd.

One night when it was all over or beginning to be over I was in my apartment which was about a block away from theirs. There used to be a diner that I could go to in the morning if I wanted to watch her walk to work or him take the kids to school. And I think Ted Berrigan used to sit there in that same diner after staying up all night doing speed to watch Frank O'Hara hail a cab to work. But I was alone in my apartment in this bluish winter morning. If there was anything to drink I had already drank it. The window was all fogged and I taped some pretty Christmas card to the window. It was corny but it looked really nice. I wanted to copy the window. To be in charge. And we didn't have cellphones yet. I still live in that apartment and right now in the web of vines out my window there is one red leaf that won't fall. It's stuck and I've tried to take its picture and you can't. Now it's snowing so I'm sure it's gone.

After I stuck the card on the window I just became an echo. I vanished into my situation. I think it's the opposite of dramatic. If there's a gland I've only used it twice to produce a poem. Here's the story:

AND THEN THE WEATHER ARRIVES

> I don't know no one
> anymore who's
> up all night.
> Wouldn't it be fun
> to hear someone

really tired
come walking
up your stairs
and knock on your door.
Come here
and share the rain
with me. You.
Isn't it wonderful to hear
the universe
shudder. How old it all,
everything,
must be.

How slow it goes, steaming
coffee, marvelous morning,
the tiniest hairs
on the trees' arms
coming visible.

I like it better,
no one knows

sweetness, moving your
lips in silence.
Closing your eyes all night.

It's so much better
disarming myself
from terror, and light
passing through
a painting I stuck
on a window
earlier, when I was scared.

It's great, it's really great.
Trees hold the world
and the weather
moves slow.

Even a body dissolves
and takes a place, incorrectly,
everywhere I would
like to nuzzle,
and plants a heart
in the world
voiceless.

I began knocking.
Ridiculous. Just to hear
your echo back,
arm against face

just to stop those fucking
trucks, my thoughts
of vanishing
into that sweetness.

Is it the same poem? It's the same life. The same gone person, feeling so anonymous in her love. I remember the joke Bernadette, her husband (Lewis, otherwise he would hate it) and I had which was what she said as we were breaking up: that she was no one. No I guess we had this conversation earlier when we were all in love. She was no one. I said I was anyone. He said it would be nice to be someone. So when I missed her I wrote "I don't know no one / anymore who's / up all night."

And we did stay up all night at first. Don't lovers always.

"Wouldn't it be fun / to hear *someone* / really tired / come walking / up your stairs / and knock on your door."

So he's there too. So I'm the only one that's gone. I'm the only one now up all night by herself. It's sort of like the afterglow of love is this person who can't sleep. And, yes, eventually even she has to leave and that poem is her residue. Just a puddle on the page of what she's felt.

Will this happen again. That planet took 32 years to repeat. I don't think there will be another one, not by this person. No.

Not unless my mother dies and she will. She's 93. She's the one who reminds me of both these intense orphans—alluring & abandoning I wrap my life around & then I get thrown out. This is it I'm sure. And I'm the baby ghost at the frosty window while the computer plays on. "My uncle is a tuber," texts Adam. "Spring has a belly."

He's explaining the meaning of *Maggy*. I'm that little red leaf. The storm is over and the leaf is still there. But you know what I mean. I'm directly defecting to that planet's rings.

New York, 2014

ACKNOWLEDGMENTS

I'd like to thank the editors of the journals that published the new poems: *Poetry Magazine, Cold Front, American Reader, Maggie* and especially the *Occupy Wall Street Anthology,* compiled by Boyer, Marinovich, Giron, Simmons, Sarai, Glassheim, Sheeler, Cobb, Del Corazon, Robey, Shamier and The Poets Of Occupy Wall Street, 2012.

And the Liverpool Biennial for commissioning "Twice" for their catalogue: *A Needle Walks into a Haystack: 8th Liverpool Biennial*, Koenig Books: London, 2014.

And *Transparent* for using ". . . I always put my pussy" in season two.

The original book publishers: Jim Brodey of Jim Brodey Books, Barbara Barg of Power Mad Press, Dennis Cooper of Little Caesar, Chris Kraus, Sylvere Lotringer, Hedi El Kholti and Jim Fleming of Semiotext(e) and Autonomedia, John Martin of the legendary Black Sparrow, Jack Kimball of Faux Press, Joshua Beckman, Matthew Zapruder, and Charlie Wright of Wave Books.

My best readers & this book's true friends: Maggie Nelson, Elinor Nauen, Peter Gizzi, CAConrad, Erica Kaufman, Adam Fitzgerald, and Elisa Biagini who began things a decade ago by asking for poems to translate into Italian and to each book's dedicatees: David Rattray, my mother, Joan Larkin, Leopoldine Core, Robert Harms, Bob Creeley, Jennifer Montgomery, Myra Mniewski, Jordana Rosenberg, Barb McKay, Ted Berrigan, Alice Notley & Jimmy Schuyler, and to Rose Lesniak, my original muse and Jill Soloway for knee socks like tonight.

Greatest thanks to Emilie Stewart for standing by the whole trip, to Gabriella Doob for each step, Gee Henry for vivid support and enthusiasm and finally to Dan Halpern for being my editor and for our very first conversation that reshaped and even renamed this book. All the thanks in the world.

Cover Catherine Opie 2005.

31901056621784